Across *the* River

Across the River

BHAICHAND PATEL

SPEAKING TIGER

SPEAKING TIGER BOOKS
125A, Ground Floor, Shahpur Jat
New Delhi – 110049

First published by Speaking Tiger Books, 2024

ISBN: 978-93-5447-891-8
eISBN: 978-93-5447-911-3

10 9 8 7 6 5 4 3 2 1

Typeset in Baskerville MT Std by SÜRYA, New Delhi
Printed at Chaman Enterprises, New Delhi

'We cross our bridges when we come to them and burn them behind us, with nothing to show for our progress except a memory of the smell of smoke, and a presumption that once our eyes watered.'

—from *Rosencrantz and Guildenstern Are Dead*
by Tom Stoppard

I

MONSOON 2007

1

Madhu is in a hurry.

'*Bhaiya, zara jaldi karna*,' she urges the rickshaw man, 'I'm getting late.'

The man huffs and puffs, swipes the sweat from his brows with a finger and pedals harder. She is a regular and always addresses him with warmth and politeness.

Nearing her friend Seema's lane, Madhu rings Seema and tells her to come down and meet her at the usual corner. Seema is ready, adjusts her dupatta in front of the mirror and hurries down the stairs. Once on the street, she looks up at the flat's window. Sure enough, her mother is there, above the tangle of electricity cables and wires. Seema blows Jabeen a kiss and her mother blushes.

'*Pagli*,' she whispers to herself and shouts to the daughter, 'Don't forget to call!'

Seema nods, waves and rushes on.

'I'm nervous,' she says, climbing into the rickshaw next to Madhu.

'What are *you* nervous about, drama queen?' Madhu laughs. 'You're the brightest student in the class.'

'I think I messed up some of the answers in the statistics paper.'

'You'll do fine. Bhaiya, *jaldi*, please.'

The college gate is already open when they reach. To Madhu's dismay, her plan to be the first to arrive has not worked out. They head towards the notice board. Scores of excited students are already milling in front of it.

'Wait here,' Madhu orders Seema, 'I'll look up the names.'

She is the more aggressive one and has no problem pushing and shoving the girls and boys aside with her determined 'excuse me-s'. It does not take her long before she turns to an anxious Seema, standing some distance from the crowd. She gives her a broad smile.

'You got a first!' she yells, and makes her way back to Seema. 'And me too,' she adds triumphantly. Together they shriek with joy, provoking a serious-looking young man to frown and say, 'Will you calm down? This isn't the civil service, you know.'

Madhu ignores him and turns to Seema. 'You got higher marks than me.'

'Sorry,' says Seema sheepishly.

'Don't be silly,' Madhu responds, dragging her friend towards the college canteen, 'we both knew you would. Come now, let's celebrate.'

The place is crowded and there is palpable excitement in the air. The two girls find seats on a bench at the end of a long table.

'What will you have?' Madhu says, taking charge.

'Just coffee, thanks.'

'Nonsense, we're celebrating,' Madhu says. 'And it's on me.'

Seema knows better than to argue. It has always been left unsaid that her friend's family is richer. Madhu returns with coffee and a plate of pakoras which she sprinkles with a generous amount of chilli flakes.

They have been there about half an hour, before Seema's eyes are drawn to a man at the door in greasy overalls, anxiously looking towards them. He is accompanied by the college security guards. She recognizes him now. The man is one of the employees at her father's workshop. Right away Seema knows that something is wrong.

No one in the family was aware that Zafar Chaudhry had a weak heart. He never had it checked, although his weight should have been a warning sign. He was under a car parked outside his repair shop, tightening a bolt when the spanner dropped from his hand with a clank. An alert assistant found Zafar on the ground, sweating and breathing heavily. They pulled him out and one of the employees ran to fetch a doctor from the nearby clinic. By the time he arrived, Zafar was gone. First attack, last attack. He was not yet fifty.

2

The night before had been a sleepless one for Madhu. She had tossed and turned for hours, but when sleep finally came, around dawn, it was a deep one. The alarm kept ringing and her mother had to shake her awake.

'Beta, you will be late,' Uma—never one to raise her voice—said gently.

It always annoyed Madhu when her mother addressed her as 'beta'. For her father she was always 'beti', daughter. She knew it was a common practice in many families to call all children 'beta', regardless of gender, but still it sometimes gnawed at her. She was their only child. Was her mother disappointed that she did not produce a male heir, someone to take care of them in old age, someone to 'carry forward the family name'? But the feeling never lasted longer than a second. Madhu knew that she was overreacting. They loved her unconditionally. She often had to remind herself that she was, in fact, lucky in her parents. Had she been born in any other family of her community, she would have been married by now and probably a mother, too.

She looked at the clock and cursed. Today, of all days, she was going to be late for college. Madhu intended to be outside the iron gates before they were flung open, to be among the first to see the results posted on the board.

Pass or fail, first or third class, she did not want to hear it secondhand from anyone. Why was this so important to her? Madhu didn't exactly know, but it was.

She brushed her teeth quickly, gargled a little less than usual and did two quick strokes with the silver tongue-scraper. Then she showered and got dressed in her lucky outfit, washed, pressed and kept ready for this day. The breakfast, a slice of buttered toast with milky masala chai was taken on the run, a feat that annoyed as well as impressed her mother. Uma had cooked up a storm for breakfast—parathas stuffed with aloo, gobi, and chutneys of three different varieties—but Madhu did not touch any of it.

'Come on, Maa, hurry up.'

The mother refused to be hurried. Some things could not be rushed, and risking the displeasure of the line-up of gods in front of her was one of them. She rang the prayer bell vigorously as she chanted. The incense stick holder was overloaded today and the smoke, pleasant as it was, a bit overpowering.

Mother and daughter were in the family prayer room of the Gupta home, a little, windowless room next to the kitchen with a spacious cupboard that was over-crowded with small brass and marble figurines of gods and goddesses—Krishna, Ganesh, Lakshmi, Hanuman, Durga and the Shiva-linga—to whom the family turned for help on different occasions. While Lakshmi, goddess of wealth, the consort of Vishnu, was her husband's favourite, Uma herself was partial to Ganesh. It was him she addressed as she prayed for her daughter's success in the college results. Madhu graduating would be a first for the women of the family.

Uma put a tika on her daughter's forehead, holding the tray of lit diyas with her other hand. Both mother and daughter knew the tika would be rubbed off once Madhu was on the streets.

'Hurry up, Maa,' said Madhu again and Uma frowned. Madhu whispered a sorry, for she loved her mother too much to disrespect her gods. Besides, she was on the fence herself when it came to religion. She certainly did not want to displease any god and invite misfortune.

Not far from where Madhu lay tossing and turning a few hours ago, Seema also awoke at her home in the walled city of Old Delhi. Family lore had it that their ancestors from her father's side were part of the entourage that moved with Mughal Emperor Shah Jahan when he shifted his capital in 1628 from an overcrowded Agra to more spacious Delhi.

At that time the head of the family had a high rank in the imperial court and the family's new home in Delhi, a haveli, had a formal garden—with a fountain!—where deer roamed and peacocks danced. This, at least, was the family legend. The Yamuna lay on the other side of the wall of their compound and, it was said, the family's felucca was docked a few steps down the steps. They used it for sailing and in good weather would picnic somewhere on the riverbank and a retinue of servants would be sent ahead to make preparations.

That was then. The family fortune declined over the centuries and by the time the last emperor was exiled to Rangoon, their glory days were long over. They could no longer afford the haveli. It was sold to the British army for a pittance and later demolished to make way for a housing estate for officers and their families.

Now Seema's family occupied a two-room flat above a row of small shops and dhabas in a lane close to the grand mosque in the walled city. To reach the flat one had to climb an unlit staircase that was seriously in need of repair. Above the flat was a terrace that was exclusive to it. On hot summer days and nights, it was a godsend to the family, air conditioning being a luxury beyond their reach. They had a desert cooler, but given the water supply in their locality—an hour in the morning and even less in the evening—that too was a luxury.

On cold winter nights the staircase was used by street people as their sleeping quarters and the family did not have the heart to turn them away. Seema and her family were careful, going up or down, not to step on the sleeping forms. On particularly bitter nights Jabeen sent them hot chai in kulhars.

Jabeen, Seema's mother, came from a line of zamindars from Azamgarh. The family had converted to Islam in the seventeenth century. It was the time when Vikramjit, the Rajput ruler, changed his name to Azam Khan and gave the district his name. By the time Jabeen was born, the family had lost most of their land, but there was still enough to live with some dignity, if not comfort. Jabeen's parents grew maize and owned a mango orchard. They had seen better times, but the rundown family house in Azamgarh was spacious and comfortable.

Jabeen's was an arranged marriage and she had not seen her husband before the nikaah. The baraat, a modest one, had come by train from Delhi. The two were distant cousins. If she was disappointed on first setting eyes on the somewhat cramped living quarters in Delhi, she had the grace not to show it. Her husband, Zafar Chaudhry, was a loving man and a good provider, and though they had their struggles, it was a happy marriage.

Seema and Madhu lived within the crumbling walls of the old city, just a couple of hundred metres from each other, but in worlds that were far apart. The two girls had been the best of friends since their first year in college. It had begun when they found themselves seated next to each other on the first day. Theirs was one of those colleges where girls tend to stick together to avoid sniggers and malicious gossip.

The day they first met, both were nervous and somewhat excited. They made small talk and slowly a friendship developed. Both girls were in salwar-kameez and dupatta every day, like most girls. Seema also wore a hijab, not an uncommon dress form in their college. So it was never in doubt that she was Muslim and Madhu Hindu, but that hadn't mattered to either girl.

Some may have found their friendship unusual, thinking they came from milieus so different that they could only be like aliens to each other. But they weren't, really. They were kindred spirits, both from conservative backgrounds but with open minds themselves.

The girls who came to college wearing jeans and sometimes skirts were a breed apart. They came from posh neighbourhoods of the city, compelled to attend this unfashionable college abutting the old city, and a stone's throw from the notorious red-light area, because of poor grades. It is also reasonable to assume that some of their parents feared they would get mixed up in wrong company in some other college and, horror of horrors, end up marrying outside the community or caste. Perhaps they thought there was little chance of that sort of corruption in this sedate, 'backward' college.

Because of its lineage, conservative Muslim parents also preferred sending their daughters to this college. When the campus of Delhi University was developed soon after Independence, a plot in the north of the city was given to the college, but the management could not be persuaded to move. The college remained in the crowded, down-market part of the city. But while it may have been unfashionable, its success rate in final university exams was remarkable.

Seema and Madhu had joined the ranks of the 'bright' students within weeks of joining the college. And through the three years of graduation, they were inseparable. On pleasant, sunny days they would open their lunch boxes and eat together on the college lawns. A few years back the authorities had put up a high brick wall to discourage gawkers. One of the college employees was also tasked with shooing away hungry kites and crows while the students lunched. But there were occasions when a determined kite would swoop down and grab a sandwich or poori right from the hands of an unsuspecting student.

Sometimes other girls joined Madhu and Seema, but most times the two preferred their own company. The boys did not even try. Madhu brought aloo pooris, stuffed parathas and spiced chhole while Seema's mother often packed kebabs and biryanis. The first time Madhu offered Seema her tiffin, Seema had refused politely—as is the norm. But Madhu persisted.

'Please take some. My mother has packed more than enough.'

Seema scooped the aloo with a bit of poori and took

a bite. She pronounced it delicious, before offering Madhu some kebabs from her small plastic lunch box.

'I'm a vegetarian,' her new friend had said, apologetically.

'Sorry, I should have asked.'

'No need to be sorry. I didn't ask you whether you eat aloo. I should have. I know people who hate aloo!' Madhu laughed.

After that, whenever her mother made something special, Madhu asked her to pack extra for her friend. While Madhu would not touch the kebabs and the biryanis, she loved the desserts Seema's mother sometimes packed, perhaps leftovers from some celebration the previous evening.

3

Katra Premnath Rai Marg is a rather grand name for what is essentially a lane with pretensions. It begins at Chandni Chowk and meanders its way south towards the grand mosque, the Jama Masjid. Auto-rickshaws that have replaced the horse-pulled tongas are allowed along the route but, for some years, it has been off limits to cars. For several years now, there've been signs prohibiting honking but no one pays attention to them. When something heavy is to be delivered it is done on carts pushed and pulled with grunts by sweating men. Small trucks carrying supplies to shops are permitted at night after nine when the lane, presumably, goes to sleep.

It is here that Madhu lives with her parents.

Madhu's mother, now in her early forties, was barely eighteen when her parents got her married to a boy not much older than her. Aroon, the boy, was not only of the same caste but also of the same sub-caste. Uma did not have to change her Gupta surname when she married.

It had been a happy marriage, both of them would have been at a loss if you asked them when they last had a major quarrel or serious disagreement. They divided the work evenly; she took care of the home and he of the business. There was always enough cash in the Godrej steel almirah in their bedroom for Uma to use as and when she wanted. Only on important matters would they huddle and decide together.

Uma had not received much of an education. After her matriculation, she was pulled out of school by her parents, as were most girls in their bania trader community. She had learnt to read and write and do basic math, which was all that was required of the girls. Her two brothers ended up with college degrees. Uma was envious, a bit resentful, but took that as normal. Things were not very different in the family that she was soon married into. Aroon had two sisters, who had both been married off when they were sixteen.

Unlike their parents, however, Uma and Aroon were determined to give their only child a proper education, let her break out from the confines of the community. In their separate ways, both Uma and Aroon—a sensitive boy who in his teens had silently loved a Christian girl he knew he would never be allowed to marry—had felt stifled by the strict rules and prejudices of their community. They did not want their daughter's life to be curtailed as theirs had been. If Madhu chose to go to university and then to work, they would have no problem even if others frowned. And frown they had, three years ago when she started college. Their relatives warned she would get ideas, she might even end up marrying outside the community. But Uma and Aroon ignored them. As a compromise, the college closest to home was selected. As it turned out, because of Madhu, the next year two of her cousins joined college too, but a women's college.

The haveli that the Guptas lived in dated back to the time before the British took Delhi, though there were no records on when it was constructed. In more recent times, it was the home of the family of Lala Chandimal, owner of an upscale jewellery shop in the fabled Chandi Chowk bazaar, a brisk ten-minute walk away. At one time the Chandimal's had Nawabs and Maharajas as customers, though the Rai Bahadurs—a title bestowed by the British on Indians who furthered the cause of the Empire—bought more and haggled less.

Some years before Madhu's grandparents moved into the haveli building, the Lala's college-educated children had persuaded him to buy a plot of land on Rajpur Road in Civil Lines, where they built a modern bungalow with spacious lawns. It had become a trend among the wealthier lot of Old Delhi, especially Hindus and Christians. Living in the walled city became unfashionable once motorised vehicles replaced the ubiquitous tongas. The cars found it difficult to manoeuvre the narrow lanes and what was once a tranquil place became a cacophony of shouts, incessant blowing of horns and occasional bouts of road rage. The exhaust fumes added to the misery.

The Lala and the wife were never happy in the new home and, had it not been for losing face with their previous neighbours and the reluctance of their children and their wives, they would have happily returned to their beloved haveli, whatever the disadvantages. For sentimental reasons the Chandimal's retained ownership of the vacant haveli but when the old man died sometime in the mid-1970s, his children sold it to a developer who converted it into eight independent flats with newly-added bath-and-toilet facilities. He gave the building a new name: Hari Kunj.

The neighbourhood was a community of like-minded people, almost all vegetarians, mostly Hindu with a sprinkling of Jains, and that is how it was in Hari Kunj—decent, middle-class families, six Hindu and two Jain. A family that intended to boil an egg in the kitchen would not be able to buy a flat in Hari Kunj.

Four of the flats were on the ground floor around a common courtyard, and four on the floor above. Two narrow staircases, facing each other across the courtyard, led up to these flats. Old men and women huffed and puffed as they climbed up the stairs. Some had to be carried up by family members, and some others had not ventured out in years. At one time there had been an agreement on installing a lift, with the costs shared four ways by families living on the first floor. A company came to look into the possibilities and decided it would be possible only if they took space from the courtyard. The ground floor residents vetoed the proposal and nothing came of it. There was bad blood among the residents for some time before the matter faded away.

The women in the haveli liked to gather in the courtyard in the afternoons after the chores were done, to while away the time and gossip. They took turns making the chai. They returned to the flats after an hour or so to prepare for the return of the husbands from work.

Leading into the courtyard from the lane was a massive door through which an elephant could pass with ease. It was kept open twenty-four hours, with a chowkidar posted at night for security. When it was closed one could assume that there was tension within the walled city. Riots were rare in these parts, but rumour sometimes rode the air, especially at election time.

Passers-by in the lane had a clear view of the courtyard through the open door and sometimes foreign tourists requested permission to enter and take a closer look at the old haveli. This invariably caused excitement among the women who were at home. They looked down into the courtyard from above or discreetly from behind curtains if they were on the ground floor. They retreated quickly if the visitors' eyes turned towards them. Whatever elegance the haveli and the neighbourhood might once have had, was now gone but the structure itself remained solid and imposing and some of the carvings on the doors and windows had survived the builder's modernizing zeal.

All the eight families in the repurposed haveli got on well, though most of the time they kept to themselves. At times of crisis or loss, however, they were there for each other. If a special delicacy was cooked, it would be shared with a neighbour or two. During Navratri celebrations they jointly put up a mandap and for nine evenings they feasted and fasted together. At Diwali, they would light up the place with diyas and exchange boxes of mithai.

When there was a death, the bereaved family did not light a stove for days. The neighbours took turns bringing food and helping with whatever rituals needed to be performed.

Gossip floated up and down the lane and reached Hari Kunj as well, and there would be whispers, but in public most of the families would be discreet and pretend not to have heard anything. In any case, much of the gossip was harmless talk of the goings on in the gali's households, with the dhobi and milkman being the main culprits. There were few secrets in the neighbourhood.

Four of the families in the haveli were owners of shops within walking distance. Among them were two Gujarati brothers who occupied flats next to each other.

The older brother, Mangalbhai, had a shop in Kinnari Bazaar, five minutes away, that specialized in procuring and selling zari threads made of gold and silver; but the bulk of his business was from sales of cheap threads that resembled gold but were silk, cotton and polyester yarns mixed with copper. His supplies came from his hometown of Surat. His two employees were distant nephews from impoverished farming families. They slept in the shop after the shutters were down.

Customers ordered these threads from as far as Benares but most of Mangalbhai's business was from owners of modest looms on the outskirts of Delhi or in one of its satellite towns. They turned up in person at the shop, sat cross-legged on gaddas, as Mangalbhai did himself, and negotiated prices over cups of chai. On hot summer days they were offered lassi from the street seller down the lane who churned it fresh in a large matka. Some of the buyers used the trip as an excuse to have lunch in Gali Paranthe Wali that connects Kinnari Bazar with Chandni Chowk. Legend has it the gali was established in the seventeenth century and it was the idea of Jahanara Begum, daughter of the Mughal emperor Shah Jahan. This may or not be true but the story was, and remains, good for business.

The younger Gujarati brother, Ranchhodbhai, ran a private courier service from the crowded Cloth Market at the furthest end of Chandni Chowk, close to the railway station, that buzzed with activity. Most of his customers did not know how to fill out a Federal Express or DHL form. While parcels and letters were accepted, the main business was of transferring money from one Indian city to another. Ranchhodbhai specialized in sending and receiving cash from Gujarat and Mumbai.

There were several 'angadia' services like his that operated from shabby hole-in-the-wall offices in the back alleys of the old city. The looks were deceptive; together, these cubby-hole establishments were a conduit to the daily transfer of tens of lakhs, sometimes crores, of rupees belonging to traders. Diamonds were also transported by them to and from Surat, the largest hub in the world for polishing these precious stones. The couriers were indistinguishable from other passengers in the second class on express trains. The valuables were tied, sometimes glued with tapes, to their bodies, and they travelled in groups to provide each other protection.

For their regular customers the angadias were also willing to transport items like Alphonso mangoes from Valsad, a variety favoured by Gujaratis who are known to extract the juice, add ghee and crushed garlic and consume it as part of a meal.

The owner of another ground-floor flat in Hari Kunj had a shop selling light fixtures in Bhagirath Palace, the largest retail and wholesale market for domestic electrical items in Delhi. One would have been hard pressed to find his shop in the maze. The address didn't help either, but you only had to mention the name of his establishment to any shopkeeper in the noisy warrens and he would point the way. The shopkeepers helped each other out this way; there was enough business here for everyone. It was the kind of market where the seller was surprised if you did *not* bargain.

Madhu's father, Aroon Gupta, was a silver merchant in Dariba Kalan—'Street of the Incomparable Pearl'—which connects Chandi Chowk to the grand mosque. He specialized in antiques and heirlooms. He was known for his honesty and people from distant parts brought their precious possessions to him for evaluation, knowing they would get a fair price. Usually, these people were desperate for money—illness in the family, marriage of a child, business not doing well—and would be parting with something precious and of sentimental value to them. Aroon was a kind man and it did not occur to him to cheat them.

His buyers were sometimes walk-in customers attracted by a piece displayed in the window—like old, ornate silver picture frames, which sold almost as soon as they were put on display. Sometimes these walk-in customers were tourists taking in the old city on foot, and they would often buy old silver coins with images of Queen Victoria or George V. Most of Aroon's buyers, however, were regulars, some of them collectors of antiques, others owners of shops in posh neighbourhoods of New Delhi—Sundar Nagar and South Extension—who resold the antiques with a handsome mark-up.

Aroon's was the only family in Hari Kunj with a single child and one of only two with a girl. This demographic was either a strange design of nature or the result of illegal sex-determination clinics that abound in North India. All the children in Hari Kunj, even those who had turned adults, followed the conservative habits and customs of their elders. But unknown to the parents, many of the boys had developed a taste for chicken. Mutton, fish and pork would have been taking things a bit too far. They sneaked around in groups to the dhabas in the Muslim section of the old city, close to the grand mosque where they could conceal themselves in the crowds, knowing there would be hell to pay if their parents found out.

Unlike vegetarianism, a common bond among the families, the prohibition against liquor was less strictly enforced, at least among the adult men. Some of the homes had a bottle or two of Scotch in the cupboard, supplied discreetly by the neighbourhood bootlegger. His prices were lower than those of the government run liquor shops. It was always Scotch, not the local stuff and the preference was for Black Label. On late Sunday afternoons some of the older men got together for drinks over a game of *teen patti* with low stakes. The game moved from flat to flat every week, with the lady of the house taking care of the namkeen and pakoras. The whole business was discreet; nobody got drunk. One of the unwritten rules was that no man, no matter how old, would drink or smoke in the presence of a family elder.

The neighbourhood had its advantages. It was safe. The few robberies that had taken place turned out to be inside jobs. Women felt protected and everyone greeted each other on the street. There were always four youngsters to carry a body to the crematorium when the time came—sometimes even a young Muslim neighbour would volunteer to be a pall-bearer, although Hindu and Muslim families almost never had a meal in each other's homes. The prayer meetings that followed on the fourth day after the death were always well attended.

At times of a marriage everyone lent a helping hand, putting up the mandap, serving food and generally seeing to it that everything went like clockwork. If money was short the father of the groom or bride could get a loan from one of the neighbours without feeling embarrassed.

However, the glory days of mohalla living were fast becoming a thing of the past. For many years now, this hadn't been a fashionable place to live. Its reputation fell even lower after new cars and gadgets, cable TV and international fast-food chains began to arrive in India in the 1990s. Often, college-going children were embarrassed to invite friends who lived outside the walled city to their homes. Every few years, when a family prospered or needed more space, it moved out, at the urging of the children. The housing colonies that had come up across the river in the eastern part of the city became popular destinations.

When a move was happening, everyone in the building got together in the courtyard at the time of departure. The women shed tears and promises were made to keep in touch, though they were seldom kept.

In Hari Kunj, though, all but two of the flats were still occupied by the children and grandchildren of the original owners. Among them were Aroon, Uma and Madhu.

Seema's family lived a brisk fifteen-minute walk from Madhu's home if one avoided rush hour when the roads were chock-a-block with vehicles of all shapes and sizes. Demographically, though, there was a sea change between the two neighbourhoods.

Until the 1940s, the walled city was home to a number of prosperous Muslim families, but many of them left for the new country created for them upon Independence. Two of these well-heeled refugees went on to become presidents of Pakistan.

The poor Muslims did not have the luxury of taking that plunge into the unknown. And so the character of the old city changed. Some of the now vacant Muslim havelis were sold for a pittance, others that were abandoned were allocated by the authorities to refugees coming from the other side of the new border.

Over time, some of these Old Delhi families that had prospered a little moved to newly constructed flats in Okhla in South-east Delhi, close to the Yamuna river. The population of this idyllic semi-wilderness had grown gradually since 1935, when a university was established here to offer education to Muslims in particular. It had never been easy for Muslims to find accommodation in mixed housing, so Okhla became a ghetto.

Seema's family had not moved from the walled city. Until his death, her father, Zafar Chaudhry, had been the manager of a car and motorcycle repair shop not far from their home. It was a modest enterprise with just about room for a desk and an old telephone, but it served its purpose. Most of the repair work was done on the street with the connivance of the police who turned up at the end of the month for their bribe. Besides Zafar, there were two employees who did minor repairs, fixing tyres, replacing wipers, smoothening dents. They were not allowed to touch the car engines. That was Zafar's domain. Some of the customers came all the way from posh parts of the city where they would have had to pay almost double for similar services. Zafar had the knack of finding locally made spare parts that were just as good as those supplied by the car's manufacturer but cost half the price. The more expensive the cars, the bigger the savings.

Zafar was an employee, the owner of the repair shop was a man who had several other businesses and rarely visited the workshop. Zafar had been promised partnership, but he died waiting for it to happen.

Seema was a month short of her twenty-first birthday when Zafar's heart gave up. Her brother, Rashid, was fifteen. He was precious. Jabeen had him after two miscarriages. With his baby fat gone and puberty well underway, he had developed movie-star looks—Salman Khan without the muscles. He had even been offered a small modelling job, the family was tempted but eventually turned it down.

Rashid's school, just outside Ajmeri Gate, was three hundred years old and had started as a madrasa founded by a general in Aurangzeb's army. When it went through hard times, the East India Company reorganized it and in 1828 named it the Anglo Arabic School and added English to the curriculum. Though it had among its notable alumni the first Prime Minister of Pakistan, Liaqat Ali Khan, by the time Rashid joined it, the school was not known for its quality of education, unlike the school where Seema was sent—Queen Mary's College, just outside the northern gate of the walled city, which came under the aegis of the Diocese of Delhi, the Church of North India, an offshoot of the Church of England.

Rashid's grades were consistently disappointing, but he had turned out to be a genius with computers and everything electronic. The whole neighbourhood came to him with their broken appliances and there was never a gadget that he couldn't fix. If someone needed a new computer or cellphone, he would check the prices on the internet and send them to shops in Nehru Place where they were likely to get the maximum discount. After they'd bought a computer, they brought it to Rashid to check that the original parts had not been replaced with cheap knockoffs. All this Rashid did for free.

On some days, when Rashid returned from school there was a queue of people waiting for him. It did not escape Jabeen's notice that more teenage girls, some even in burqas, were turning up with their computer problems than boys. She was amused and did not comment, but Seema would tease him and he would go red in the face and stomp off, swearing never to speak to her again.

4

When she is given the news of her father's death, a shocked and bewildered Seema rushes home with Madhu. A crowd of mourners has already gathered at the flat, with some people overflowing to the terrace above and the street below. A few are relatives of the deceased, but most are neighbours and people Zafar had known through his workshop. When Seema arrives with her friend, a path is cleared for her. She recognizes some of women as her mother's friends. They hug her and she quickly goes to her parents' bedroom. Jabeen howls when she sees Seema. Tears flow without pause and mother and daughter embrace. Rashid too has been summoned from school.

Madhu squats next to Seema and cries silently. She had grown fond of the kind, unassuming man who struggled but was always smiling. She calls her mother to break the news. Her parents arrive shortly afterwards and pay their condolences. Soon, the visitors who are in the bedroom leave to let the family grieve in private. Early that evening Madhu too rises to go but Seema pulls her back.

'Please stay,' she says.

Madhu rings her mother and asks her to send over her night clothes and toilet kit with the maid.

The burial is fixed for the next day, unusual under the

sharia, to give time for Jabeen's relatives to arrive from Azamgarh. The body is washed by her older brother, Javed Ahmad, and her cousins soon after they reach Delhi. It is wrapped in a white shroud and left in the living room for friends and relatives to pay their last respects. Jabeen and the children say their final goodbyes and after a collective prayer the body is carried down the flight of stairs. The women wail, some because it is the tradition to do so.

After the burial at Qabristan Ahle Islam, those who have come from the village stay the night at Jabeen's flat. The daughter vacates her room for her uncle, Javed, and aunt. She sleeps on the bed in her parents' room with her mother, while Rashid sleeps on a mattress on the floor. The other guests, all male, are accommodated on the living room floor on borrowed mattresses. The evening meals for everyone come from one of the dhabas in the neighbourhood at no charge. The next morning, except for Javed, the visitors take the train back home.

Javed stays for a week, receiving visitors who come to pay their respects. He sorts out the family's estate—what little there is—with everything going to Jabeen and the children. Fortunately, the flat is owned by them and free of encumbrances. Javed tells his sister that he will take care of the household expenses henceforth but Jabeen will have none of it. The evening before his departure, Javed asks his sister and niece to join him on the terrace.

'You can't stay here, you know that,' he tells his sister as he watches, with some pride, the floodlights being turned on at the imposing Red Fort in the distance. 'You will all come to the village and live with us.'

Mother and daughter are surprised by this development. Before Seema can say something out of turn, Jabeen asks her to go down and see if Rashid has gone to bed. Seema is not happy but does as she is told. A minute later she returns to the terrace but stays at the door. Jabeen nods to her; a sign that she can listen from there.

'Bhai jaan,' Jabeen says softly, 'Seema has just completed college with a first-class degree. What will she do in the village? Besides, Rashid is in an English-medium school. He's good with computers and will find good employment…'

'They will have a better life in the village,' Javed interrupts her. 'It is your home. The land and house was left to both of us by Abba.'

Although not wealthy, the Ahmads are well-to-do landowners. Javed has always felt that his sister could have done better than Zafar for a husband but kept that opinion to himself. It was an arranged marriage through relatives and despite the struggle, it had been a happy one.

Jabeen's eyes fill with tears. A part of her wants to honour her brother's love and say yes.

Javed has been taking in the view of the Red Fort while he spoke. Now he turns to his sister.

'Who was that girl yesterday with Seema?'

The question surprises Jabeen.

'You mean Madhu? She's Seema's closest friend. They've been in the same class in college for the past three years.'

'Is there a shortage of girls of our community in Delhi?'

Jabeen finds the remark distasteful but says nothing.

'What will you do here?' Javed continues. 'This place is a dump compared to what we have in the village.'

An awkward silence follows before the brother speaks again.

'Zafar had life insurance. It should help for a while.'

'Zafar was a good provider,' the sister says, 'we lived comfortably.'

'How much is there in the bank?' Javed asks.

'A little over twenty thousand rupees.'

It is Seema who has responded from the terrace door. She keeps the accounts for household expenses. At the end of each month her father would hand his month's pay to her. She would keep some cash for the bills and household expenses and deposit the rest in a savings account for which she was a co-signatory.

'Well, how long is that going to last? It's settled then. You will all come back to the village. The children are my responsibility now.'

Jabeen is alarmed. She looks towards her daughter who is in tears.

'Bhai jaan, be reasonable. Rashid has no future there, you know that,' she says politely, but with firmness. 'Besides, Seema is now a graduate and wants to work. We'll manage.'

'Where will she find work? What kind of work?' he asks with irritation. 'No. It's decided. You will return to your family home. This city is no place for a woman alone. You should start packing. Sort out everything, I will return in two weeks to take you all.'

He has spoken with a cold finality and he immediately regrets it.

'The village is not what it used to be,' he adds a little gently. 'We have factories nearby, good boys, graduates with jobs. How old is Seema? It's time we looked for a husband for her. Besides, what's all this nonsense about Seema working? Women in our family have never worked.'

Jabeen looks towards the door. Seema is now standing in plain sight, shaking her head. Jabeen pauses before she speaks again.

'Bhai jaan, I know you mean well. You are a kind person.

You have always helped us. The children always look forward to coming to the village during the holidays. But living there permanently?'

She pauses again, gathering her thoughts.

'Give me six months. I will try and get Seema married and settled here. There are some nice boys, educated and from good families. If things don't work out, we will do as you say.'

The brother relents.

'All right. Have it your way. You have six months here. No more.'

He turns around and looks towards the Red Fort again.

'What a beautiful city this was when we ruled over it. Chandi Chowk was the envy of the world. There was nothing like it in all the world. We built it. Hindustan during the Mughals was richer than any country in Europe. Now look what these grass-eaters have done. The city is one big slum.'

He stays on the terrace for a long time, while Jabeen and Seema go back to their room. Seema hugs her mother and whispers: 'Thank you, Ammi.'

Next morning, after her brother leaves, Jabeen finds a thick envelope filled with money beside her bed.

5

A few weeks after the examination results, Seema is going through the Sunday paper's classified section with its matrimonial ads (grooms seeking 'homely' girls), new flats for sale, and job vacancies.

Madhu is stretched out on the bed next to her friend. She is turning the pages of a book she has picked up from the college library at the recommendation of her history teacher. Strictly speaking, this is against the rules since she is no longer a student, but the librarian made an exception on the understanding that the book would be returned before the start of the next academic year. From the library card, Madhu noted that the book had not been issued in years.

'What are you reading?' Seema asks for conversation's sake, without the slightest interest.

'This is interesting,' Madhu perks up. 'Did you know our college is over two hundred years old? It says here that it was established by the British. Let me quote: "to uplift the uneducated and barbarous Indians".'

'Obviously they did not succeed.'

'Shush! There is more. One of the men behind it was Lord Macaulay. He was the guy who declared that, and I quote again, "a single shelf of a good European library is worth the whole native literature of India and Arabia".

'He actually said that?'

'Yes. And then he spent his time in India establishing an educational system based on the British model.'

'Well, bad people end up doing some good, I suppose. Despite themselves,' says Seema. 'But forget him. Look, here's a vacancy that seems promising. "Reputed guest house in Lajpat Nagar looking for attractive girl as receptionist and telephone operator. Flexible hours. Five figure salary." You want to apply?'

'Chhee!'

'Yes, I didn't think so.'

Madhu's mother enters the bedroom with glasses of lassi in tall steel tumblers.

As usual, the lassi is laced with powdered almonds and so thick that Seema uses the accompanying spoon to scoop out some. Madhu takes the newspaper from Seema and reads from it.

'I think I will apply for this one. "Exclusive bar in Gurgaon is looking for bright young girls to work as hostesses. Transport provided. Five figure salary with generous tips." Yes, this one sounds good. I will apply.'

Uma yelps in shock. 'What!'

'Stop it, Madhu. Aunty, your daughter is teasing you.'

'Don't even joke about such things,' Uma says. She turns to Seema. 'Beti, stay for lunch. We're having chhole puri.'

Uma knows that it is the two girls' favourite comfort food.

'Yummy! Thank you, Aunty. Let me call Ammi and tell her not to wait for me,' Seema says.

'How is your mother?'

'She is okay, Aunty. She's being brave for Rashid and me.'

'Trust in God, beti. And support your mother, she is a good woman. Tell her I will drop by in a few days.'

'Please do, Aunty. She will like that,' Seema says and Uma caresses her head and blesses her. '*Bhagwan ki kripa rahe tum par beti.*'

Basking in her warmth and affection, Seema feels certain that God's grace would indeed be hers.

Jabeen is on her Singer sewing machine, which she had brought with her when she married and moved to the city. She turns the wheel with her right hand and feeds the cloth to the needle with her left. Her husband had offered to buy her an electric one but she was quite content with her old faithful. Now, especially, she finds that working on it relaxes her. Although she is only in her forties, her eyes are not what they were, and when she has difficulty passing the thread through the sewing needle, she beckons whoever is at home.

'What are you doing?' she asks Seema who is sitting at a low table with her second-hand computer, keeping her mother company.

'Applying for a job, Ammi,' Seema replies.

Jabeen is taken aback. So, Seema was serious when she was going through the English papers borrowed from a neighbour a few days earlier.

'Beti, you don't have to work. I'm getting enough stitching work to keep the place running.'

This is true. Soon after Zafar died, the family's tailor had come to see her and asked diffidently if she could help—he was overwhelmed with orders and it would make his life easier if he could pass on some of the work if she could handle it.

'I'm getting on and my son is not interested in this line of work,' the man had said unconvincingly. He knew Jabeen owned a sewing machine and he knew, too, how radically things had changed for the family after Zafar's passing. He was a kind man and Jabeen was touched by the offer.

So there was some money coming in. It wasn't a lot, barely enough for their everyday needs, and an additional income would improve things immensely. But Jabeen worried about her daughter going out into the big, bad world. How far would she have to travel? What kind of people would she have to deal with?

Seema's voice pulls her out of her thoughts.

'What do you expect me to do, Ammi? Stay at home all day? I will go crazy. Quite a few girls in our mohalla now have jobs.'

Jabeen sighs.

'Your Mamu will be furious if word reaches the village, as it surely will.'

'I don't care. I'm not going to that village, whatever happens. Once I start earning enough for us, I'm sure Mamu will leave us alone,' Seema says.

'I wouldn't take that for granted.'

Seema gets off the auto-rickshaw and looks up to see the building on Kasturba Gandhi Marg. She is at the right address. Madhu had tried to persuade her not to wear the hijab, but Seema was determined to wear the headscarf—as she usually did in public.

Whatever impression the building gives from its rundown facade and its accordion-like elevator door, the office on the fourth floor is plush. It takes up the entire floor and is carpeted. The receptionist asks her name and then tells her to put down her details in the visitor's book, her address and contact number and the name of the person she has come to see. Seema wonders why this is necessary but does as she is instructed. This is her first job interview and if she is nervous, it does not show.

The receptionist finishes polishing her nails, picks up the phone daintily and makes a call. Then she tells Seema where to go. A peon is waiting on his chair for her outside the cabin, he gets up as soon as he sees her and opens the door for her.

'Sir, Miss Chaudhry,' he announces and shuts the door behind her as she enters.

The personnel manager is busy going through the file before him. He takes his time, does not look up but gestures for his visitor to take a seat. Seema senses it is her file.

'Give me a moment,' he says.

The man finally looks up. He does a double take seeing Seema in a hijab but, to his credit, recovers quickly. He adjusts his tie.

'Would you like some tea?' he asks, and rings a bell below his desk.

Seema declines politely, as he knew she would.

The manager decides that there is no point in wasting either his time or hers. He takes another look at the file he had pushed aside earlier.

'I see that you have a first-class BA. Good marks,' he says. 'It's very impressive. But we are looking for someone with a B.Com degree. The vacancy is in our accounts section.'

The advertisement in the Sunday paper had not mentioned that, but Seema lets it pass. She cannot help wondering that if this is the case, why was she called for an interview in the first place.

'Sir, my degree is in business administration and accounting was my main subject.'

The man fixes his stare on the file in an effort to avoid looking at the person seated in front of him.

'Yes, I see that. But that is not enough. The responsibilities involve more than that,' he replies without elaborating.

He closes the file.

'We will get back to you,' he says politely, 'We are interviewing a number of applicants.'

Seema gets up, thanks him and as she closes the door behind her, she hears him speak to someone on the phone: 'A burqa! In this office? What do these people think? Please screen people before you send them in.'

She feels humiliated and walks swiftly to the elevator. A part of her wants to go back and tell the man that he is an ignorant fool if he doesn't know the difference between a burqa and a hijab. And what is his problem even if someone does wear a burqa? She wants to ask the man if he has a similar opinion about people coming to work sporting a tilak or turban. But she knows it will make no difference. Besides, she does not feel she would have the courage to confront him.

At the bus stop outside, she is suddenly aware of people staring at her.

And so it goes. Seema keeps sending neatly typed applications, with all the required attachments. She is called for interviews several times in New Delhi as well as in Gurgaon and Noida. She continues wearing her hijab and it becomes undeniably clear to her that her showing up with her head covered leads to shorter interviews. Her name is mistaken for a Hindu one when the application is sent. Then they see the headscarf.

At the interviews she hears frequent excuses for why she cannot be given the position. After a while she tires of hearing the vacancy has already been filled. Most times the look on the interviewer's face when she enters gives the game away. To be fair, she tells herself, there are also occasions when there are good reasons why the job is not for her. But she also knows that more often her religious identity is the only reason.

To Seema's distress the family's savings are running out. As the account keeper in the family, she does not let on and Jabeen continues to meet their day-to-day household expenses through her earnings from sewing work. Three months have passed since her father's death, and she's growing worried that her Mamu will turn up unannounced one of these days.

Meanwhile, Madhu has received several offers and has finally settled on a position of responsibility in a garment factory across the Yamuna in Noida. It is in the accounts department, with a cubicle of her own. The perks are good. There are several interviews with the top management before the letter of appointment arrives through e-mail.

Despite his relatively progressive views, Madhu's father is in two minds about Madhu getting employed but her mother is supportive. Secretly, she is hoping their daughter will find a suitable boy from a more forward-looking bania family than the ones in their restricted circle.

Noida was developed to avoid the chaos that would have resulted from the rapid, unplanned expansion of the capital. Over a hundred villages were bulldozed to make way for posh residences and modern industrial areas. The owners of the houses and villages were paid a pittance. The major incentive for such a large enterprise was the amount of money the politicians and bureaucrats could squeeze out of the developers and deposit in their Swiss bank accounts, if they were clever; or stuff into mattresses, if they were not. The idea was to build a new world-class town, but in reality, it had grown haphazardly to become one big unplanned urban sprawl.

The garment factory that has hired Madhu is in a relatively less crowded and chaotic sector of Noida. She takes a cycle-rickshaw from her lane to the Red Fort or Golcha bus stops, a bus from there to the busy ITO intersection, and another one from there to a stop barely five minutes from the factory. On good days, it takes her just under an hour to make the journey.

The garment factory takes up most of the ground floor and has a gym and cafeteria. The idea of a gym on the premises had come from a foreign client. He had persuaded the owner that it would raise morale and increase production. He had probably not anticipated the fact that its use would be restricted to white-collar staff.

Unlike most garment-making factories, this one is air-conditioned and the workers are required to wear overalls. They are even given individual lockers to keep their clothes and other personal belongings. The working conditions are good, imposed by the representatives of buyers from big department stores in the West who turn up unannounced for inspection. Stories of exploitation in the international media have brought a sea change in the running of factories that relied on foreign markets.

The administrative offices of the factory are on the floor above. There are small cabins for the senior managers and large ones, with attached toilets, for the owner and president, Kantibhai Mehta, and his son Mohan, the CEO. The rest of the staff have cubicles or sit in open-plan areas.

The food in the cafeteria for management staff is several notches better than what is available on the factory floor below. The toilets for the white-collar staff are western style. There is a sign in the men's toilet requesting users to lift the seat when urinating. Many ignore it, unwilling to touch the toilet seat. The finicky South Indian Brahmins are the worst offenders.

On the factory floor, the toilets are Indian style, and no larger than cubby holes, to ensure that the workers finish their business quickly and rush out for air.

Two months into her job, Madhu is occupied on the computer when she overhears the conversation in the cubicle next to her.

'So, you are leaving us?'

It is her supervisor, Manohar Swamy. He's talking to a young man, smartly dressed, who is standing diffidently in front of his desk. Mr Swamy is a kind man with humble beginnings who has risen in the ranks of the company over the years.

'Yes, sir. I have found employment closer to home,' the young man says.

Madhu's ears perk up. She gets up from her seat to hear them better and peer over the partition.

'And no doubt, the pay is better?' Mr Swamy says with a smile.

'It's a more senior position, sir.'

Mr Swamy gets up and shakes the young man's hand.

'Congratulations. Keep in touch. And take care of yourself.'

Madhu takes a discreet look at the man as he is leaving. She has recognized the voice but wants to be certain. It's a guy who also works in accounts. Madhu gives the matter a quick thought and walks over to Mr Swamy.

'Sir, may I speak to you?'

'What is it, Madhu?'

'Sir, I couldn't help overhearing your conversation. Is there a vacancy coming up in accounts?' she asks.

'Yes, Sunil is leaving. Good man. I'm sorry to see him go. Do you have someone in mind?'

'I have a friend from college. She has a first-class degree in business management and she majored in accounting.'

'Why don't you speak to personnel? I will tell them you are coming over.' Mr Swamy picks up the phone. 'If she works out, we won't have to advertise the vacancy.'

That evening Madhu and Seema go to Bengali Market for chaat. It is quite a long walk from the old city but they decide to give it a go. The monsoon season is beginning and it is a pleasant early evening with clear skies.

'My treat,' Madhu says, nimbly picking up and examining the food-stained menu.

'Wow, a big spender!' Seema teases her.

Madhu takes out a wet tissue from her purse and gives the table a rigorous wipe, as she says, 'Wait till you get your first job. It will be your treat and it won't be here. I want Chinese at the Hyatt.'

'I'm afraid you will have to wait a long time.'

Both girls order golgappas and aloo tikis. Bengali Market, one of the oldest in Delhi, has nothing to do with Bengal or Bengalis. It was named after a gentleman named Bangali Mal. The change in spelling of the name over the years was inevitable as was the addition of that quintessentially Bengali dessert, rosgulla, on the menu of the market's most popular eating place.

After the first golgappa goes down, Madhu cuts to the chase. She tells Seema of the opening that has come up in her office. She has already spoken to HR and they have agreed to hold back on advertising the position.

'They won't take me, I know.'

There is more frustration than sadness in Seema's voice. By now she is seriously worried the family will have to move to Azamgarh.

Madhu gently suggests that her friend go to the interview without her hijab.

'I will not do it,' Seema says firmly, even though the thought has crossed her mind several times.

'Why not?'

'Do you know what you're asking? It is like admitting I'm a second-class citizen in my own country,' Seema says. 'Besides, Ammi will kill me.'

'She won't. Besides, she need not know,' Madhu says. She then tells her friend that she has already fixed her an interview at the company. All Seema has to do is turn up for it in a saree or salwar, minus the hijab.

'You leave home in the hijab and come to my place and change into one of my sarees. Even better than salwar-kameez for an interview in the office where I work.' Then she stops. 'But you've probably never worn a saree.'

'Of course I have,' Seema protests. 'Now you're being like the others. Many Muslim women wear sarees, you know. This isn't Pakistan. Though even there a lot of them do. Have you heard of Iqbal Bano, the great ghazal singer? When General Zia banned the saree in Pakistan, she went to a concert in a black saree and sang Faiz's *Hum Dekhenge* in protest.'

'Oh good,' Madhu says. 'I'll help you choose one that's appropriate for the interview. Not black, and nothing too bright either,' Madhu says, then adds, 'And please don't wear a hijab as protest, okay? We don't have a Zia here yet. And we need the job.'

Seema bows her head theatrically. 'Your wish is my command, ma'am.'

'*Shabaash*,' says Madhu, laughing. She feels relieved.

The worst part comes when they are back on the street waiting for an auto-rickshaw. Madhu musters the courage to tell her friend something.

'The factory owner is a bigot,' she lets out.

Seema smiles. She has been through this before.

'Look, we need to make this work,' Madhu says. 'He won't know. Seema Chaudhry could easily be a Hindu name. It *can* work.'

'And what happens if I get the job?' Seema asks.

'We'll cross that bridge when we come to it.'

Madhu takes her friend's hand. 'Give it a thought. Please. It's better than being dragged to some godforsaken village in Bihar.'

'UP,' Seema corrects her.

'Same difference.'

Both shudder at the thought.

'I have not stepped out of the house without my head covered since I was a child.'

'Many Muslim women wear modern clothes. I may have got it wrong about the saree, but this much I know,' Madhu says. 'As for Aunty, she'll get used to it. You once told me the hijab was your father's idea, not your mother's.'

6

The day before the interview, Madhu opens her almirah full of sarees for all occasions. Some of the sarees have been in the family for generations, heirlooms rarely worn by Madhu. The mother has passed them on to her, though on special occasions, she borrows one from the daughter.

'Take your pick,' Madhu says to her friend.

Seema is astonished by the collection.

'I have no idea. You pick one for me.'

As Madhu selects one, she says, 'One of these will be my wedding gift to you.'

'Right. It will be a big hit in Azamgarh,' her friend says sourly.

Madhu pulls out an understated Maheshwari saree—cotton with a hint of silk, so that it does not balloon out when a novice wears it. It is elegant and not dressy.

'This should be just right for the occasion.'

She helps the reluctant Seema drape it. The two look at the result in the full-length mirror.

'Fabulous,' Madhu says.

Seema is not so sure. 'I don't know if I can carry it off.'

'Don't worry. You won't have to wear it every day. Just once. After the interview tomorrow, you can wear what you like. But no hijab. We'll have to make that compromise, Seema.'

Her friend nods. Then she adds, 'I will go for the interview, Madhu. But, if I'm asked, I will not lie.'

'I don't want you to,' Madhu says. 'Now stop thinking so much about it. Come here in the morning and change. Ma will help you.'

'What time is the interview?'

'Eleven. Don't be late.'

This is the first time Seema has crossed the bridge over the Yamuna and come to Noida. It is a different world altogether—crowded and chaotic but in a large, intimidating and messy way. The warren of galis that is Old Delhi is crowded too, but in an intimate way and there is nothing chaotic or unsettling about it.

She is nervous about the interview and wants to get it over with as quickly as possible. She has no expectations. If this works, great; if not, well, she's been through this before.

She has splurged on an auto-rickshaw, not wishing to risk arriving late by bus. Besides, she didn't want to ruin Madhu's saree in a jam-packed bus. When she had flagged down an auto near the Red Fort, the driver had warned her he would charge her double for crossing the border. She had been puzzled by the mention of a border, but soon realized that although Noida was less than an hour from the centre of Delhi, it was in a different state, UP.

Now, as she gets off the auto, she is impressed by the building in front of her. She adjusts her saree before she enters the iron gate that has a brass plate with the company name polished to perfection.

Her appointment is with the president of the company

himself, Kantibhai Mehta. That doesn't help her nerves. Madhu has warned her about him. The mirror on the way up in the lift allows her to check her saree one last time.

The firm's manager of human resources is waiting for her when the elevator doors open. He introduces himself, says a few kind words by way of greeting which calm her nerves. He has been through this drill many times. A gentle knock on the door and they are facing Kantibhai, who is sitting behind an enormous desk, bigger than any she's encountered in her previous interviews.

'Sir, the person we have shortlisted for the vacancy in the accounts department is here for the interview,' the manager says. In most companies he would have taken the decision on a post opening up at this level. At K&M (Pvt) Ltd things work differently. Kantibhai is a hands-on owner.

'Good morning, sir,' Seema says brightly, folding her hands in greeting. The nervousness is ebbing.

Kantibhai looks up from the file before him and motions to her to take the chair across the table from him. The manager who accompanied her is not invited to sit. He stands a few steps behind the applicant, diffidently. Kantibhai flips through the file once more. Watching him, Seema feels that he couldn't really be the monster she had imagined. He has the face of a kindly neighbourhood uncle.

'Seema Chaudhry?'

'Yes, sir.'

'I see that you have been recommended by one of our employees, Madhu Gupta. That's something in your favour,' he says. 'How do you know each other?'

'We were in college together, sir.'

'She is a good employee, works hard and is popular with the staff. If she says you are suitable for the post, I have no hesitation in trying you out.'

She seems to have created a good impression. So far so good.

'Besides, your college grades are impressive.'

Kantibhai looks beyond her and addresses the manager.

'Have you informed her of the salary?'

'Yes, sir. It was in my letter to her.'

'Is it acceptable to you?' Kantibhai turns his friendly gaze back to Seema.

'Yes, sir.'

He speaks to the manager again.

'Are there any other applicants?'

'We have yet to advertise the vacancy, sir. But a few of our employees are interested in the post.'

Kantibhai takes another look at her application.

'Let us introduce some fresh blood in the company,' he says. 'I see you are from Delhi 6, Miss Seema. Are you close to that masjid?'

'Yes, sir.'

Is this a trick question, she wonders.

'I had a relative living near Moti Cinema. Be careful. There are lots of Muslims in that area. You never know when they will create trouble,' Kantibhai says, like an elder giving calm advice.

Seema does not say anything.

'What are her assignments?' he asks aloud.

'She will look after the factory workers' payroll and health benefits, sir,' the HR manager replies.

'Good. I am sure you can handle that, Miss Seema. That means you will observe the factory floor hours. You will come in at ten in the morning and leave at six. In case you are needed after that, you will be paid overtime. Does that suit you?'

Seema's plan of commuting to the office with Madhu is clearly not going to happen.

'Yes, sir,' she replies.

'So, it is settled. You can start on Monday.'

He turns to the HR man.

'Put her on a six-month probation.'

Then he turns to Seema.

'Nothing to worry about,' he says to her, 'that's our standard practice. I am sure everything will work out.'

The meeting is over. Seema and the HR man prepare to leave.

'By the way, Miss Seema, you are a Chaudhry. I take it you are not a vegetarian. This is a vegetarian office and factory. We do not allow meat in any form on the premises. I hope that is understood.'

'It is not a problem, sir.'

The impatient Madhu is standing near the elevator waiting for the interview to be over. Seema smiles and gives her a thumbs up.

'I knew you would make it, I'm so happy,' she says. Then, after the HR manager has asked Seema to report a little before ten on Monday and collect her appointment letter from him, and when he has walked a sufficient distance away from them, Madhu whispers to Seema, 'He didn't find out, did he?'

'No, but I'm still not comfortable with this,' Seema whispers back. 'How long can we continue with this charade?'

'Don't be stupid,' Madhu says fiercely, but still keeping her voice low. 'Do you want to be married off and waste away in some backwater? This is a harmless lie. Try and live with it. We will cross whatever bridge there is to cross if we ever come to it.'

On the first day at work Seema chooses a cotton kurta-salwar and hurriedly gets dressed. She puts on the hijab and is at the door, about to leave the house.

'Bye, Ammi!' she shouts.

Jabeen is cooking in the kitchen and rushes out.

'Wait, I am packing lunch for you.'

Seema looks at her watch.

'Ammi, I can't be late on the first day. There is a canteen in the office. The food is subsidized. I'll eat there every day with Madhu. You have enough on your hands already to worry about my lunch.'

'But I made roti and kebabs—'

'*Meri pyaari Ammi*,' Seema says and gives Jabeen a quick hug. 'Keep the kebabs for me. I'll eat them as soon as I'm back.'

Seema hurries down the steps. She boards the bus on the main street of Daryaganj, heading south. As luck would have it, it is a new private bus that goes all the way to the sector in Noida where her factory is located, a short walk from the bus stop. The bus is packed, but she manages to get standing space when some passengers get off.

She removes her hijab and puts it in her bag. A man standing next to her glares in disapproval. Seema's eyes well up with involuntary tears. An elderly woman in a burqa notices the man's glare. She gives up her seat and pushes her way to Seema. She gently puts a hand on her shoulder and says, 'Don't worry, beti. Sometimes we have to do what we have to do.'

Seema is assigned office space on the factory floor. It is airy, with a window overlooking the office garden. A maali comes and spreads feed on the manicured grass for the birds and they chirp in delight. There is enough and the kites and crows don't bully the smaller birds. She tries to open the window to take a better look but it is permanently shut for security reasons.

There is a note of welcome on her desk signed by Kantibhai himself, together with an invitation to the conference room for an orientation course. There are three new people there, besides her. One of the managers explains the layout of the building. Another speaks on the products and policies of the company and who does what. All three newcomers take notes or pretend to during the two-hour briefing that includes a slide show. When it is over, there is a complimentary lunch for them in a private room adjoining the cafeteria where some senior managers join them.

In the afternoon Seema has a one-to-one briefing on her assignment in her office by the personnel manager, followed by a walk through the factory floor. She is introduced to the workers under her supervision, more women than men. It is altogether a pleasant, productive day. Madhu has finished an hour earlier but waits for her and they take the new bus home together, chattering all the way.

The factory cafeteria is run by a chain that has several restaurants in the capital region. It is rent free and that keeps the prices of items down. There is a long self-service counter where one can pick up sandwiches, samosas and other snacks as well as soft drinks. At the further end are two cooks who make dosas and pooris on order or ladle out curries and daal to go with rotis or rice made in the morning and kept warm. Those who bring food from home can pick up plates, cutlery and napkins.

Technically, the cafeteria it is not off limits to wage earners on the factory floor but none of them ever come here. They have their own eating place on the ground floor. The food in both places is the same, from the same kitchen. The prices are a little lower downstairs, the furnishings are basic. Some of the radicalized executives prefer to go down and eat there, rubbing shoulders with the working class.

On Seema's second day at work Madhu takes her to the cafeteria. They see an empty table by the window and go and occupy it. Madhu pulls out a plastic food dabba from her bag and lays it on the table. Seema gets up.

'I didn't bring anything from home. I will go get something.'

'Silly woman! Sit down,' Madhu says. 'There is enough here for both of us. Maa always over-packs, have you forgotten?'

She gets up and brings two plates on a tray and the two dig in.

'I didn't know how to tell Ammi not to pack the kebabs and non-veg stuff she often makes for me.'

'Just tell her the factory is vegetarian and meat dishes are not allowed on the premises. Aunty will understand.'

Seema looks around.

'Are all these people vegetarians?'

'My guess is that most are not. Did you read the recent survey about the food habits of Indians? I think it was by the UN. Apparently, most Indians, even Hindus, eat meat—not just fish and eggs but also chicken and mutton.'

Madhu puts a paratha in Seema's plate, and as she spoons out some aloo sabzi from her tiffin, she says, 'You know, some of the people you see here are also undercover Muslims.'

Seema is alarmed until she sees Madhu smiling and realizes that she's being teased.

'It's not funny, Madhu. The more I think about it the more I realize I shouldn't have listened to you. I'm not at all comfortable with this.'

'Come on, yaar. Stop worrying. What will happen if the old man does find out? All he can do is fire you. Though I doubt he'll risk that. You could take him to court. Even if the law lets you down, you only have to make that kind of thing public and he'll lose some of his foreign clients.'

Then Madhu changes the subject.

'How did the briefing go yesterday? In all the excitement I forgot to ask earlier.'

'It was all right. I think I can handle it. But I wish we could travel together.'

'I'll talk to my contacts in personnel to find out how soon you can get a transfer to another department so that our timings are the same.'

'Great. But don't do that just yet, please,' Seema says. 'I like working with these workers. Sometimes I wonder how the families survive with the kind of wages they take home.'

7

A few weeks later Madhu and Seema are walking back from lunch in the cafeteria when they see a young man, in his mid-twenties, coming towards them. He is smartly dressed, and stands out from everyone else at the factory.

'Hi,' he greets Madhu pleasantly as they cross paths.

'Good afternoon, sir,' she replies with a polite smile.

After they pass, the young man looks back and sizes up Seema, trying to be discreet about it.

'Who was that?' Seema asks.

'That's the boss's son, Mohan,' Madhu whispers. 'He's been put in charge of production and has an office next to his father. Cute, na?'

The next day, a Friday, Seema is sitting at a desk outside her office, handing out wages to the workers who have lined up, as they do every Friday at three. An assistant sits next to her. The payment is in cash in envelopes with names already written on them. There are separate queues for men and women. The assistant asks for the name and digs out the envelope from a bunch arranged in alphabetical order. The employee signs—some offer thumb impressions—and Seema hands over the envelope.

Nearly all the employees are older than Seema and she shows them due respect. She has a kind word for the ones she recognizes from their visits to her office. If she is aware of an illness in the family, a death or a crisis, she takes some time to talk to them when she hands over the envelope. At first the assistant is surprised but after a couple of weeks he gets used to this and realizes that the queue does not mind the delay, a break from the tedium of factory work.

This Friday Seema is distinctly aware that someone is watching her from one of windows on the floor above. She looks up and the face disappears. Perhaps she imagined it.

Mohan has backed away from the window, embarrassed.

The monsoon has begun in earnest and it has been pouring for days. The drains clog with garbage. Seema is drenched as she wades through the foot-deep muddy water to the bus stop near the factory. Her cheap folding umbrella is of little use in this downpour. She adjusts her dupatta and pulls out a handkerchief from her purse to wipe her face as she waits under the crowded bus shelter.

It is the evening rush hour and several buses, fully loaded, pass without stopping. A Mercedes passes the stop, brakes suddenly, reverses. It is Mohan heading home. He has seen Seema drenched and rolls down the window on the passenger side and leans over, shouting to get Seema's attention. She doesn't hear him with the sound of the rain beating down and the honking traffic. A woman next to her taps her shoulder and points to the man in the car.

'Get in,' Mohan shouts in English. 'I will drop you.'

He leans across and opens the door on the passenger side by way of invitation. The people at the bus stop are now staring at Seema. Will she or won't she? She is deeply embarrassed. She shakes her head.

'I'm going your way,' he insists, 'you are drenched and will catch a cold.'

She takes a few steps to the Mercedes.

'Thank you, sir. I will take the bus,' she says politely. 'You don't know where I live.'

Mohan grins sheepishly. A bus has arrived behind him. The bus driver honks. Mohan doesn't move.

'Please get in.'

Seema shakes her head vigorously. She moves back to where she was standing earlier. Mohan does not move. The bus driver keeps honking, now impatiently. A middle-aged man comes towards the car. He takes a threatening tone with Mohan.

'Stop bothering this woman, you scoundrel! You people think you can do what you like just because you have money and big cars?'

Now other men move towards the car. There is menace in the air. Seema realizes that things are getting out of hand. She quickly gets into the car, giving Mohan an angry look. She has never sat in a car this big and luxurious but it makes no difference to her foul mood.

The Mercedes was a surprise gift from Kantibhai on his son's twenty-first birthday. Mohan had accepted it gracefully, though he would have preferred a Mini or a BMW. Mercedes was passé and he knew some of his friends would tease him endlessly about his ride. But it is almost four years now and he's got used to it.

'Where do you live, Seema?' he asks.

She does not respond, still seething. The car is now gliding forward, a cocoon of comfort in the din of traffic.

'How do you know my name?' she asks after some time, looking not at him but resolutely out of the window.

Mohan is silent.

'Drop me across the bridge, please. Somewhere near ITO,' Seema says.

'Seriously, I can drop you home. I'm in no hurry.'

Now it is Seema's turn to respond with silence.

'So, you don't want me to know where you live?' Mohan is smiling as he turns to look at her.

Seema does not answer. Mohan wipes the smile off his face. She keeps looking ahead. Mohan now realizes his mistake, he should not have been so insistent.

'Okay. ITO it is.'

At the ITO intersection he gets out of the car and opens the door for Seema. It is still raining. Seema bangs the car door behind her and without saying anything or looking back at Mohan, walks away, without bothering to open her umbrella.

'Sorry,' Mohan says. But no one is listening.

Seema waits for a bus at ITO for fifteen minutes before realizing that with so many people in the queue she will not get one anytime soon. The roads are now even more flooded, with no sign of the rain letting up. She decides to walk home, even if it takes as much as an hour.

Next morning, when she arrives at the office Seema finds a bouquet of yellow roses in a vase on her desk.

'Mohan sahib had it delivered,' the office peon volunteers.

She reads the two-word inscription on the card—'Sorry. Mohan.'—and dumps the lot in the bin. Even the ceramic vase, a rather nice one, is not spared.

At lunch break Madhu and Seema are walking towards the cafeteria.

'So, you got a bunch of roses from your admirer.'

Seema is still in a foul mood. 'What? Does the whole office know about it?'

'Pretty much. He's the boss's son, after all. Lucky you!' Madhu is laughing.

'Shut up!'

Madhu opens her tiffin box to share with Seema. They both become aware that people are stealing glances at their table. Some are whispering. Seema turns red with embarrassment but says nothing. She is determined to avoid tears.

Madhu is now concerned for her friend. 'Let's leave,' she says and both get up. 'It's sunny outside. We'll eat on the lawns.'

8

Seema is sitting at her desk when a clerk enters and hands her an envelope. She opens it and takes out the cheque. She looks at the amount and smiles. Her first pay cheque, and it's substantial. Her mobile phone rings. It is Madhu.

'Dinner tonight, remember?' she says. 'I will pick you up at eight from home.'

'I don't know. That's late. Ammi is not going to like it.'

'Leave that to me. I'll talk to her,' Madhu insists, 'I know her better than you. It's your first pay cheque and time to celebrate.'

Seema is at her dressing table, the one her father made for her on one of his days off when she began college. She has dressed for the evening out in jeans, but with a dressy kurta. She's putting on the lipstick that Madhu gave her earlier that day, when Jabeen enters.

The mother is surprised.

'Lipstick?'

'Come on, Ammi,' Seema says. 'Many of your friends' daughters, right in our neighbourhood, wear it. What's so wrong with it?'

'Have it your way.' The mother is not too concerned. She takes the lipstick from her daughter's hand after she has finished and examines it with curiosity. 'Revlon,' she reads with some difficulty. She turns it and smiles when the glossy stick moves up.

'Where are you going?' she asks.

'I don't know. Madhu will decide. I think it's a Chinese restaurant in a mall.'

'I don't think I have ever eaten Chinese. Will it be halal?'

'Ammi, please.' Seema is more exasperated than annoyed.

'Anyway. Whatever it is, you know best.'

'Ammi, all meat in Delhi is halal because all butchers are Muslims,' she says. 'And by the way, even Chinese restaurants will make sure the waiters tell you a dish has pork before you order it.'

Seema takes out her hijab from the drawer and puts it on. The mother is pleased.

'Don't be too late.'

The doorbell downstairs rings.

'That's Madhu, I'm off.'

As Seema rushes out, she knows her mother is worried. And Jabeen is, but she's also inwardly proud that her daughter has earned her first salary.

As soon as the girls are in an auto, the hijab goes into Seema's bag.

'Where are we going?' Seema asks.

'To a nightclub.'

Seema is alarmed.

'I told Ammi we're going to a mall for Chinese.'

'Well, it *is* in a mall,' Madhu says with a smile, 'and I'm sure they'll have something Chinese. They all do.'

The autorickshaw is not permitted to the mall entrance,

so the two get off on the main road, a short walk away. The elevators are at the far end of the ground floor. One of them is exclusively for the top floor. Madhu presses the button. She is almost as nervous as her friend but is better at hiding it.

When they emerge from the lift, they see a queue of young men and women behind a thick velvet rope. They wait and hope they'll pass muster and be let in; most will return home disappointed. It is the one of the most exclusive nightclubs in town, after all. Rumour has it that it is owned by a Bollywood superstar.

The usual bouncers stand sentry, muscled up with dangerous levels of steroids and in tight black tees. A man in a black suit is standing at the door with a clipboard. He decides who to let in.

Madhu ignores the queue, and goes straight to the man and gives him her name. He checks his list and lets them past the barrier without a question asked. He even smiles and bows his head just a little. Madhu is impressed. But Seema is in a mild panic. This is not what she was expecting.

'Take them to the VIP room,' the man in the black suit tells an assistant who opens the door. A blast of deafening music hits the two girls as they enter. Seema looks at Madhu quizzically: Where are we? What's going on? Madhu says nothing. She smiles and squeezes her friend's hand to reassure her.

The club occupies a good part of the top floor of the mall. Despite the huge chandelier and disco balls above them, it is quite dark, and most of the light comes from the illuminated glass dance floor. Though it is early, there are a few couples already on floor.

The assistant leads them past the bar and up a short flight of stairs with a torch to guide them. Another bouncer opens a door and lets them in. The two enter timidly into a new world.

'Let's leave,' Seema says. This is totally out of their league.

'Let's not,' Madhu replies with a mischievous grin.

As the door closes behind them the noise level comes down. Seema sees him first. Mohan is sitting by himself on a lounge seat. As soon as he sees the two women he gets up. 'Come.'

It's a command from Madhu.

'Why is he here?' Seema now senses some plot engineered by Madhu.

'He's the one who's invited us,' Madhu replies.

Before Seema can say anything, Madhu moves towards Mohan and her friend has no option but to follow. Now she understands why they got past the velvet rope with such ease. Mohan greets them with a smile and asks them to join him.

'What will you have to drink?' he asks.

'A single malt for me,' Madhu replies, 'and a gin and tonic for my friend.'

Mohan is taken aback. Seema is speechless.

'I'm kidding,' Madhu adds quickly. 'We'll both have regular coke, please.'

There is already a single malt with ice cubes in front of Mohan. Too late! He realizes he should have got rid of it before the two arrived. Madhu looks at the glass, more out of curiosity than disapproval. She picks it up and takes in the aroma, a new sensation for her.

'Don't tell anyone at the office,' Mohan says, 'if my dad finds out I'll be in deep trouble.'

The assigned waiter passes around the canapés, smoked salmon with capers on pieces of bread, vol-au-vents and various salted nuts. Lots of plump, garlicky olives are already in a bowl on the table. The two girls stick to salted nuts, something familiar.

Seema has not relaxed a minute since they entered. Madhu turns to her.

'He has something to say to you.'

Now Seema's suspicions are confirmed. She has been set up.

Before she can react, Mohan speaks in a rush: 'I'm really, really sorry. I behaved very badly at the bus station.' He pauses, clearly nervous. 'And it was irresponsible of me to leave the flowers on your desk.'

So, she was brought here by Madhu to hear an apology. Seema is too fond of her friend to be angry. And he seems genuinely contrite.

'It's fine, don't worry,' she says softly, barely audible. 'Though the flowers were a bit much. You embarrassed me at the office.'

She looks around, still not comfortable in the place. She turns to Madhu, 'I'm going to the ladies' room.'

Mohan suppresses a smile at her use of the old-fashioned term.

'I'll come with you,' Madhu says and accompanies Seema to the other end of the hall, guided by a waitress, an elegant woman from the North-east.

On a door at one end of the hall is a neon-lit image of bright red lips, provocatively parted. The waitress opens the door for the two friends and steps back.

Nothing so far has prepared them for what they encounter. As soon as they enter, they are greeted by the sight of a massive reproduction of a Khajuraho carving that makes them blush. The ceiling is covered with Italian-style frescoes. The walls are painted a bordello red. Unlike the rest of the club, the bathroom is brightly lit, and a mirror lines the entire length of one wall. The taps are gilded; everything reeks of money.

As soon as Seema reaches to wash her hands, a female attendant steps forward with a hand towel that smells of jasmine.

Meanwhile, Madhu has decided against using the toilet. When she opened a cubicle, she found two women, bare-breasted and locked in an embrace. She backed away quickly.

When they're walking back, Seema asks, 'What's all this about? You told me we were going out to celebrate my first salary cheque. What is he doing here? I didn't know you two were friends.'

'We're not exactly friends. Until now I only saw him around the office. I've never had a serious conversation with him,' Madhu says. 'He saw us together at the office some days back. He rang me and told me what happened between you two. He realizes his mistake.'

'So?'

'He wanted to meet you outside the office and apologize. He can be quite persuasive.'

'And he is the son of our boss,' Seema says, 'so you arranged this?'

Madhu nods.

'Idiot!' her friend says. Madhu is relieved. Seema has calmed down.

'It's okay,' Seema adds, 'I just wish you had warned me.'

'You wouldn't have come then,' Madhu says. 'He suggested this place. I've only read about it in the papers, and I was tempted to see it. I've seen more than I had bargained for.' She tells Seema about what she's seen in the toilet.

'Well, maybe they'll remember to lock the door next time,' Seema says, trying not to appear shocked.

They take their time walking to the lounge seats, in no hurry to join Mohan.

'I've never seen anything like this. Now that we are here, let's enjoy ourselves,' Madhu says.

'Ammi will have a fit when she hears of this.'

'Mine too. So let's keep this to ourselves,' Madhu says. Then she adds, 'He's cute, though, don't you think?'

Seema blushes, but can't help smiling.

Later, on the way out of the lounge, Madhu helps herself to a few pieces of candy from one of the bowls on the table and puts them in her bag. Seema too is tempted but thinks better of it.

9

In the weeks that follow, Seema proves her worth to the company. Her supervisor is impressed. After two months she asks if she can change her office hours.

'Do you wish to move to the office floor?' he asks.

Seema is surprised. That was not her intention.

'No, no sir, I like my work here. It's just that I live in Delhi and the commute would be easier if I came at nine in the morning,' she replies. 'There are more buses running at rush hours.'

Approval from HR takes a couple of days but permission is granted on the understanding that on Fridays, pay day for the employees, she will stay till six instead of five. Now the two friends travel to work and back together.

On Fridays Madhu waits for Seema. That is the evening the two spend together, sometimes by themselves and at other times with a couple of friends from the office.

Many of the employees are also young and single. Some live with their parents in modest high rises in Noida while others from the provinces share flats in the DDA colonies. Some have paying guest accommodation close to office where guests are discouraged. On Fridays they meet after six somewhere for drinks and dinner and return to their homes at a reasonable hour.

Mohan calls Madhu and invites her and Seema to a movie and dinner the following Saturday.

'I'll get back to you,' Madhu replies, non-committal.

She checks with her friend. Seema agrees and suggests the four o'clock screening at a South Delhi mall and maybe a coffee afterwards, but no dinner.

Once she is out of the house that Saturday afternoon, Seema puts the hijab in her handbag. It is an outing with two friends, nothing more, she tells herself.

A few more lunches and movies follow over the next three weeks. Madhu begins to suspect that Mohan's feelings for Seema are deeper than she had imagined, this isn't a passing infatuation, and she is concerned. Sooner than later, he will have to be told.

Two months later, Mohan and Seema go for a movie alone in the afternoon. Afterwards she takes the bus home, refusing the ride in his Mercedes. At the office they avoid each other.

They are in the cafeteria. Madhu is shovelling food from her tiffin box onto Seema's plate and her own.

'What's up?' she says. 'All okay?'

Seema is surprised by the abrupt question, but doesn't show it.

'Lots of work piling up on the desk, yaar,' she replies.

Recently she has been working late in the office and taking the bus home alone in the evenings.

'You know what I mean, Seema.'

'What?'

'I love you, my *jaan*. Don't get bruised. This is not going to work. Your Ammi will never allow it, and there's also your mamu. As for Mohan's father…' Madhu shudders at the thought.

Seema is silent for a few seconds. 'We are just friends,' she says.

'Are you sure about that?' Madhu asks softly.

Seema's eyes sting, she turns her face away from her friend.

II

1954–2007

10

Kantibhai's father, Mahendrabhai, had come to Delhi in the mid-1950s from Nadiad, an overgrown village in central Gujarat that considers itself a city. It was once ruled by Muslims, then by the Hindu Maharaja of Baroda. Temples and ashrams abound in the town, and like most residents of the town, Mahendrabhai's family lived and breathed religion, next only to commerce.

The family dealt in tobacco. The sandy soil of the district and moderate rainfall being ideal for the plant, the leaves that the Patidar farmers grew in the areas surrounding the town were of high quality and ended up in cigarettes rather than beedis. In the 1930s, Mahendrabhai's father and uncle began to buy the dried leaves from the farmers and send them at a small profit to a cigarette maker in Hyderabad where they ended up in packets of ten, labelled Char Minar, by all accounts the cheapest cigarettes available in India. It was popular with those who had gone upscale from smoking beedis, as well as a growing number of college students. As the orders from Hyderabad grew, Mahendrabai and his older brother joined the business.

However, they were not the only suppliers to the factory and competition was tough. When their margins got too narrow to support everyone, the younger brother decided to branch out. Mahendrabhai wrote to one of his maternal uncles who had established himself as a cloth-seller in Delhi to see if he would take him on as an apprentice, with possibility of employment if things worked out.

The uncle was hardly in a position to refuse. Their subcaste was small and the fiercely loyal community had a tradition of helping each other. If one were travelling one could expect a meal from a total stranger, even a bed sometimes. There is, to this day, a small directory, updated every few years, with names and addresses of members of the subcaste spread across the globe.

Mahendra was newly married and he left his seventeen-year-old bride behind in the care of his brother until he settled down in Delhi. He promised the family that if things didn't work out, he would return to Nadiad.

The uncle in Delhi had sent instructions on how the young man could reach his home in the cloth market in Khari Baoli. It was within walking distance of the Old Delhi railway station and he would have no trouble finding it if he followed the directions. He wouldn't need a tonga.

Mahendrabhai got off the train when it halted at the New Delhi station. No one had told him that the *Frontier Mail* he had boarded in Baroda would stop twice in Delhi before heading north. It was a legendary train, the most famous in the country, which once ferried British soldiers and civilians directly from the Ballard Estate port in Bombay all the way to Peshawar on India's then North-west frontier. Young Mahendra should have got off at the station after New Delhi, the Old Delhi Railway Station. He realized his mistake only when he asked someone for directions to Khari Baoli. A station employee advised him to take the next train heading north from the same platform and get off at the first stop.

The uncle and aunt had begun to worry when Mahendra didn't show up at the expected time but they were relieved when he arrived at their doorstep before long, with his steel trunk and bedding.

To make place for Mahendra in the business, the uncle had to dismiss one of his employees. To start off, Mahendra would not be paid a salary, he would have to learn the ropes. It was a modestly successful business, but the shop was barely big enough to swing a cat. The uncle sold bolts of cloth wholesale, one of dozens of shops in the ancient market with cobblestones. The customers, all retailers, went from shop to shop and drove a hard bargain.

Mahendra stayed with the family in their two-room rented flat on the first floor of the market with shared toilet facilities. He ate with the family and slept on the floor on the mattress he had had the foresight to bring with him. In the morning, he would roll up the mattress, as did the two sons of the family, not yet teenagers. Mahendra was treated almost like family, not as an employee.

The following month he was given a salary, more an allowance, of a hundred rupees. It was generous, since he did not have to pay for food and accommodation. On Sundays, the market was closed and it was his day off. He would spend it exploring the city. One day, he went all the way to Qutab Minar in a shared tonga. He saw Lutyen's New Delhi that had come up just some decades ago, and went window shopping at Connaught Circle—he was too shy to enter any of the establishments. He sat in the front stalls at Novelty Cinema, around the corner from the Cloth Market, Moti a bit further out, and the brand new Golcha on the main road of Daryaganj. It was here that he saw his first films. He enjoyed the Raj Kapoor-Nargis starrer *Shree 420* for its songs, although he did not agree with the portrayal of the big city as a place of vice and evil alone. He thought the problem was that Raju was a lazy dreamer with zero business sense; the man did not know how to do *dhanda* and ended up becoming a small-time swindler. The other film, *Miss Coca Cola*, he liked for the title and for the dancer Helen. He wondered how much the producer had managed to extract from the soft drink giant for brand promotion.

Mahendra tried to stay out of the uncle's flat as much as possible on his one day off, to give his hosts a break from his constant presence at work and in the cramped home, though no one had said anything. In fact, the two young boys became fond of him and treated him as they would an elder brother. He played carom with them and taught them the few cards tricks he knew.

Someone had told him of the vegetarian dhaba, Vig, at the Red Fort end of Chandni Chowk that was famous for its chhole puri and rosgullas, dishes previously alien to him. The price was within his range. Another spot that became his favourite was the dahi bhalla stand outside the Central Bank, halfway up the same road. One Sunday, a posh car came and parked at the food stand. A liveried chauffer stepped out, placed an order and took the dish to the car. The back window came down and a hand the colour and texture of honeyed milk, with thin gold bangles, took the plate. The window went up again and the car was driven off. Someone whispered that it was the famous movie star Meena Kumari, who was shooting in Delhi.

At his uncle's shop, Mahendra sat on a gadda, legs folded, sandals off, and took orders. The platform was a few feet above the ground, twelve feet wide on the street side and a little less in depth. The gadda covered most of it. There was a narrow iron ladder at the back, a permanent fixture, that led to the ceiling where some of the stock was held. For larger orders the goods would be fetched from their rented warehouse nearby. Customers could either order standing in the lane or climb up on the gadda after taking off their chappals if they were negotiating a serious transaction. They all wore leather chappals and many wore dhotis and white cotton caps. It was that kind of business. Steaming tea in earthen containers would turn up whether the customer wanted it or not.

Soon enough Mahendra learnt to quote prices and knew at what price to settle the sale with the bargaining customer. The regulars, however, did not haggle; they took it for granted that the price was the best that could be offered. The uncle was aware that he would lose them to his competitors if he became greedy. The business brought in modest profits but he was happy with this. The family lived comfortably and the boys went to a good school.

After six months Mahendra sent for his wife, Kanchanben, who arrived with her brother as escort since she had never travelled outside Nadiad. The brother returned the next evening, not wanting to be an additional burden on the already generous relatives.

Kanchanben was welcomed warmly and made comfortable in an alien city. A week later the couple moved into a rented flat Mahendra had found and had furnished. It was in the same market, above one of the shops.

Mahendra continued working for his uncle for another year before he branched out and set up his own shop, in a lane close by, with capital mostly sent by his brother from the tobacco trade. The uncle added to it an interest-free loan. The loan was paid back within a year. Mahendra insisted on adding a modest interest.

To avoid enticing any of his uncle's customers, some of whom he had come to know well, Mahendra chose to specialize in drapes and curtain material.

Kanchanben became pregnant soon after they moved into their flat. Her mother came a month before the baby was due to arrive. She took charge and insisted on being the midwife. It was a girl. The parents were disappointed, the grandmother even more so. But she was a sweet baby, and they soon got over the disappointment and she was loved and pampered by all.

They bought things for her they could barely afford, a jhoola as well as a folding pram. The grandmother loved massaging the baby every morning after a bath. Her strokes were gentle, and it created a bond between the two. Kanchan's mother was good at baby talk and it invariably brought out a smile.

The astrologer who was summoned examined the lines of the baby' palm and predicted a long life. Her horoscope favoured a name for her starting with the letter 'S'. They named her Sarla.

Six months later Sarla developed whooping cough. Granny had left and the mother mistook it for a normal one, nothing to worry about, and gave her small spoonfuls of cough mixture. The cough persisted and they took her to a local doctor who diagnosed it for what it was. He gave the child antibiotics but the parents had gone to him too late. The baby died.

Their next child was born a year later, early in 1958, and again Kanchan's mother came to play midwife. It was a boy, and laddoos made in desi ghee were distributed to the neighbours. This time the astrologer, his standing not affected in the least by his prediction about the first baby, declared the letter 'K' favourable. The boy was named Kanti.

The grandmother placed little Kanti between her thighs, as she would Sarla, and gave him a massage with warm mustard oil every morning after his bath.

Kanti brought the family luck, as the astrologer predicted. He had got it right this time. The business grew. The couple would have liked more children and though they tried and kept hoping for at least one more, it did not happen. But Kanti brought them so much joy, they did not mind. He was a pampered child. The flat was small and he slept on his parent's bed till he was ready to go to school. As a child of the community, he automatically got admitted in the recently established Gujarati Samaj School in Civil Lines. It was at some distance from the Cloth Market but it was several notches above the other schools in the neighbourhood. He took the school bus in the company of other children living in the area. The mother would drop and pick him up at the bus stop until he was old enough to make his own way.

The school had classes in written and spoken Gujarati but it was an optional subject in an otherwise, essentially, Hindi-medium school. The result was that after a couple of years Kanti spoke to his parents in Hindi and they replied in Gujarati. No one found this strange. All her life his mother could not quite get the hang of Hindi and her mix of Gujarati and Hindi was a source of amusement to the family and friends.

By the time Kanti was in his teens he became quite fluent in Gujarati and that was the language in which he began communicating with the family and relatives. But he struggled with reading and writing in his mother tongue all his life. His grades in school were a disappointment to his parents, but they tried not to show it. He enjoyed the summer visits to Nadiad with his mother. His cousins envied his life in the big city and loved listening to his tall tales.

There were frequent family picnics on Sundays. His mother would pack a dry lunch in a stainless-steel tiffin—puris with spiced aloo made the Gujarati way, boiled and lightly fried with methi vaghar, salt and haldi—and the three would head out in the morning for places like the Qutab grounds or the Okhla bird sanctuary. They would find a quiet spot where Kanchanben would spread a bedsheet for them to sit on. Kanti was allowed to wander around on his own while they kept an eye on him. They would catch the bus home late afternoon, after Kanti had had his favourite treat, a chocolate ice cream in a cone from a Kwality cart.

Kanti wanted to go to college after he finished high school but his father thought it would be a waste of time. His grades were a problem but, more importantly, the business was doing well and Mahendra needed a reliable help. The boy was disappointed but had no choice but to accept his father's decision. For years afterwards he felt a good education and a better grounding in the English language would perhaps have taken him somewhere quite grand.

After his school days were over, Kanti subscribed to the Indian edition of the American monthly *Reader's Digest* at a friend's suggestion to improve his English. Back in the 1970s, this 'pocket magazine' was popular among the English-educated and hoping-to-be-English-educated middle class, with its abridged versions of popular books and a vocabulary quiz, 'It pays to Build Your Word Power'. *Reader's Digest* was an easy read, even for Kanti, and he devoured each issue as soon as it arrived in the post. The part he liked best was the vocabulary quiz. Mahendra, noticing Kanti's enthusiasm at self-improvement, relented somewhat. He got a tutor who taught at a school close by to come twice a week in the evenings to teach Kanti English.

Meanwhile, the business prospered and Kanti, now a young man, persuaded his parents to move their residence from the congested and unfashionable Cloth Market to somewhere more suitable to their growing status. A housing society in East Delhi had come up exclusively for Gujaratis. The land had been granted by the government at a concessional rate. Only those with vegetarian kitchens could apply. It was left unsaid that only Hindus and those of related sects, like the Jains, were welcome.

It was one of the first private housing societies to be built across the Yamuna, and although East Delhi was not a very sought after neighbourhood then, all but a few flats were sold even before construction was completed. Mahendrabhai grabbed one of the few that were still available. The flats were modest in size and most of the other occupants were also from the crowded tenements in the lanes and alleys of the old city. They were moving up the ladder.

A few years later, through frugal living and a bank loan, Mahendrabhai became the proud owner of a small garment factory in Pitampura in the northern outskirts of the city. It specialized in women's clothes that were affordable and bought by wholesalers who, in turn, sold them to owners of stalls and carts in South Delhi markets like Sarojini Nagar and Lajpat Nagar which were frequented by the aspirational middle classes.

Mahendrabhai's 'harem pants' were particularly popular with the hippie crowd that had first begun to descend on Delhi from Europe, via Afghanistan and Pakistan, in the late 1960s, on their way to more exotic places like Kathmandu or Goa. A decade later, there were still a fair number of these dropouts, dreamers, runaways and adventure seekers passing through the Indian capital. Harem pants were as big hits with them as ganja and Osho.

The designs of these baggy trousers, with distinctive tulip-shaped bottoms, might have originated in the deserts of Africa but Mahendrabhai had stolen them from a garment maker close by. He improved the quality of the cloth and through use of cheaper labour, his prices were lower than his competitors. For a short time, he had more or less cornered the market. He ploughed his profits back into the business, expanded his factory and moved on to bigger things.

After a couple of years, Mahendrabhai was elected to the managing board of his housing society. The year he became its president, he suggested to the board that they extend an invitation to the Minister of State for Textiles in the central government to be the chief guest at the society's annual Navratri celebrations leading up to Diwali. The man was a Gujarati, Thakorbhai Sinhji by name, and recently appointed to the ministry.

Together with the housing society's secretary he took the invitation to the minister's office in Shastri Bhavan. They had turned up without seeking an appointment and the minister's private secretary was not too pleased. But he let them leave the invitation card that gave the details of the event with a note in Gujarati requesting his presence as chief guest. They did this with no great expectations.

To the society's surprise, a hand-delivered letter arrived at the housing society the next day saying the minister was delighted to accept the invitation and that he would be accompanied by his wife. There were not many Gujarati families in Delhi at the time; it could well have been that the minister was simply craving the company of people who spoke his language.

The housing society held nine days of festivities. Tickets were sold to nonresidents who wished to attend the dandiya dance in the evenings. While there was no restriction for women, men were only admitted if they were accompanied by partners. The dandiya sticks were provided but the snacks and drinks had to be purchased with coupons. The society made a tidy profit that went into its welfare fund.

It was only when Thakorbhai Sinhji arrived at the gate on the first day that the society members realized the minister was a tribal and not a Rajput as his name suggested. Not a 'pukka Gujarati' like us, some of the offended ladies whispered among themselves maliciously.

The members of the society, recovering from their initial shock, welcomed the minister and his wife with full honours. They were seated at the only table covered by a tablecloth and decorated with flowers. Mahendrabhai, as president, had the honour of sitting next to the minister. To everyone's relief the obligatory speeches were short and the dandiyas were distributed and young men and women began dancing in circles. Soon their parents shyly joined them and they were better dancers than the youngsters who soon gave up and moved to one of the ground floor flats to open a bottle secretly.

'What business are you in?' the minister asked in an attempt to make small talk at the table. His wife had not said a word all evening except for the traditional regional greeting, *kem chho*. But her smile was captivating. She was relieved that everyone was eating with their fingers.

'I have a garment factory,' Mahendrabhai said.

'That's interesting. We are more or less in the same of business,' the minister said with a smile. 'You make clothes and my ministry promotes them.'

'No sir,' Mahendrabhai protested, 'ours is a small factory.'

'I would like to know more,' the chief guest said. He pulled out a little notebook from his kurta pocket. 'Let me check…ah yes, Friday. Come to my residence at ten this Friday and have tea with me.'

'It would be my pleasure, sir,' said a rather astounded Mahendra.

Mahendra did not tell anyone of the invitation except his wife who, he had assumed, was not invited.

He arrived on the dot, but the minister kept him waiting for an hour. Not that he was otherwise occupied. He was in the bedroom reading the day's newspapers and making calls. Mahendrabhai realized soon enough that keeping guests like him waiting was customary in high government circles. He did not mind. This was the first time he had been invited to such a grand residence and by such a distinguished man.

When the minister appeared, he was all apologies. Tea was promptly brought in with dhoklas and an assortment of namkeens. The minister urged his guest to try some. The domestic help, standing by, put some of the snacks on a small plate and passed it to Mahendrabhai.

After the usual preliminaries the minister got down to business.

'My office checked, your garment factory is quite small, as you told me,' he said. 'You should expand.'

'I would like to, Thakorbhai, but finances are a problem.'

'I can help you there,' the minister said.

The government had received an order from Moscow, channelled through the State Trading Corporation, for nurses' uniforms. It was a modest order, for five hundred uniforms, but it had to be executed with almost lightning speed. The minister suspected that the Soviets were testing the waters. More orders were likely to follow, his office had told him, if they were delivered on time and made to specifications, in every detail. Moscow had large holdings in rupees that could not be converted into roubles.

'Can your company handle it?' Thakorbhai asked.

'No problem, sir,' Mahendra lied.

The minister's research had been thorough. He knew it was lie.

'I don't care how you do it, Mahendrabhai, as long as you don't mess it up.'

The minister told his visitor that they would not be meeting again. He was not to call him or get in touch with him. He wrote down a number to call if there was an emergency.

'I will send someone to meet you. He does not work for the government, he works for me. You will deal only with him.'

Manohar Pillay arrived the next day at Mahendra's factory. He was, to put it bluntly, a dalal, a variety of pimp, in this case a go-between for several senior civil servants as well as ministers. They trusted his discretion implicitly; he would not squeal. His standard commission was five per cent, less if the transaction ran into crores. It was enough to allow him to live in a tony Delhi neighbourhood and drive a Mercedes.

But he did not. He lived with his wife and two children in a DDA flat without an elevator, and drove around in a second-hand Premier Padmini. The only concession he made for himself was that his rented flat was in Chanakyapuri, on Vinay Marg, so that he could have easy access to the people he served. Nobody, except the ministers and babus he fixed deals for, would have guessed that he had a bank account in the Cayman Islands, a popular tax haven. The account was managed by his brother who lived in the US, in a working-class neighbourhood in Queens, across the bridge from Manhattan. Manohar transferred his rupee income, all cash, through the havala system. Everyone along the line took a cut, including his brother.

Manohar looked around Mahendrabhai's small factory and sniffed condescendingly. This was small potatoes. He was not used to places like these, but he guessed the minister knew what he was up to. He opened his Samsonite briefcase—battered and ancient to discourage snatchers—and extracted the specifications for the nurses' uniforms, the colour, the sizes, the design specifications as well the thread content of the cloth. He was not at all confident the man behind the desk was capable of figuring this out but that was not his problem.

Mahendrabhai went through the binders and swatches.

'Fine,' he said after a few minutes, 'when do you need them?'

It was not fine by any means, he hadn't a clue what was required. But he wasn't about to let the visitor know.

'The minister needs a sample for approval by the weekend,' Manohar said.

He handed Mahendrabhai his business card.

'Phone me when it is ready and I will come and pick it up. But no later than Friday.'

The wily man worked alone, no assistants. It was safer that way. Mahendrabhai assured him that it would be done and the unconvinced visitor left in his battered-looking car.

Now was the time to panic, and for a moment,

Mahendrabhai did just that. But he knew this was a luxury, and he forced it down and took a deep breath. Then he took a closer look at the designs. They looked simple enough, but he had difficulty understanding the specifications. Well, he would have to find a solution. There was no way he was going to lose this order.

He called a factory owner, a fellow Gujarati, who ran a more sophisticated operation and whose grasp of the English language was marginally better. They sat down together and the man wrote down everything in simple terms, part English, part Gujarati. No charge. That was what friends were for.

The sample was ready by the time Manohar came on late Saturday morning, He gave it a cursory look and was satisfied. He produced a contract from his briefcase that had all the details of the order except the price that Mahendrabhai was to charge for the order.

'Leave that to us,' Manohar said.

A few weeks later, an official letter was delivered informing Mahendrabhai that his factory had won the contract. He learnt later that the State Trading Corporation had placed a notice in a government-approved newspaper inviting bids for the contract. Mahendrabhai had no clue as to what his bid had been until later. After all the bids came in, the minister had put a bid on his behalf that was a little above the highest bidder. And he had backdated the bid. It was a scam, as Mahendrabhai would learn, and it was just the way business with the government was conducted.

Mahendrabhai was well aware he could not handle five hundred uniforms in the timeframe he had been given, but he knew someone who could—an owner of a factory who specialized in exports. He subcontracted the whole order to him without revealing the source. The man had his suspicions but said nothing.

A few weeks after the uniforms were delivered to a government warehouse, a cheque arrived from the State Trading Corporation. The day it was encashed, Mahendrabhai called Manohar, who collected fifteen percent of the amount in cash as agreed. No receipt was requested and none offered. How the cash was shared and by whom was of no concern to Mahendrabhai. It still left him with a handsome profit.

The orders kept coming after that, each larger than the last. For a year he kept farming them out to owners of bigger garment factories who asked no questions. Some insisted on being paid partly in cash. Mahendra had no problem with that.

With the windfall, he paid a deposit for land in Ghaziabad and Manohar arranged a loan with a nationalized bank. Since no collaterals were asked for, Mahendrabhai suspected money had changed hands. Within months he got the necessary clearance and the new, larger factory was soon off and running. Now he could handle whatever State Trading sent his way.

Kanti was no longer sulking from being denied a college education since life was pretty good now. He was put in charge of production at the factory and kept an eye on the accountant. Mahendra gave Kanti a brand new Premier Padmini as present on his twenty-first birthday. Kanti got himself a driver's licence without taking a driving test. One of the employees was dispatched to pick it up from Delhi's Transport Department.

Although he had put Kanti in charge of the factory, Mahendrabhai continued to handle the purchase of fabrics, linings, buttons and whatever else was required for the ministry orders. He no longer had to make the rounds, though; suppliers turned up at his office in the section of the factory that was air conditioned. Mahendra was a hard taskmaster. He narrowed down the suppliers to those who could be relied on when it came to quality and price.

The arrangement lasted while the going was good. Three years later, Thakorbhai was transferred to another ministry with full cabinet rank. But by then Mahendrabhai had made a killing. He had also had the foresight to realize that the orders would not keep coming forever and had been preparing for the day when they would dry up. He had studied and understood the needs of the foreign market, and knew there was money to be made, as long as he did not compromise on quality and as long as he could squeeze the suppliers of raw material and keep his operating costs low.

In 1976, during the Emergency imposed by Indira Gandhi, her notorious son Sanjay, the de facto prime minister, set up Noida as an industrial area. Four years later, Kanti persuaded his father to buy a small plot there. Mahendra wasn't easily persuaded. He had seen hard times and was reluctant to venture into the unknown. But eventually he gave in. There was something about Kanti's confidence and enthusiasm that appealed to the businessman in him.

He had saved enough, and with another bank loan he built a corrugated iron shed on the plot of land, with a modest concrete office block a few yards away. The first summer, the heat in the shed was unbearable and the workers were quitting one by one until Kanti, without consulting his father, got ceiling fans installed.

The company, now called K&M, expanded and went into partnership with someone who knew a thing or two about retail. Together, they opened a shop in the Chanakyapuri market, close to Delhi's diplomatic enclave, and next to the famous Chanakya cinema hall. The shop relied almost exclusively on customers from Russia and eastern Europe. They flew in from places like Moscow, Tashkent, Warsaw and Budapest with suitcases full of items for sale in India—caviar, smoked meat and small items like watches and transistors that were not available in India. On the return trip they packed the same suitcases with leather jackets that were popular but expensive in their countries. Their profits were low but sufficient since they were not primary providers in the family. As a bonus they enjoyed a short holiday in Delhi away from the harsh winters of their home countries. These men and women from the Communist block made arrangements with customs officers at airports on both ends. And at both ends the staff at the state-owned airlines' check-in counters, who were also on the take, allowed the over-loaded suitcases to go through without excess baggage charges.

Since working with leather was not permitted by his caste, Mahendrabhai set up a separate unit to make leather garments, mostly jackets with zips and overcoats with wool linings for winter use. His leather supplies came from a source on the outskirts of Kanpur where, at the time, cattle sold off or abandoned by the owners because they were no longer of any use were slaughtered and the hides sent to tanneries. There the skins were dehaired, degreased and soaked in water to be processed into leather. The arrangement worked well for seller and buyer, whether Hindu or Muslim, and everyone was civilized and professional about the whole business.

But it was a noxious business. Once, unwisely, Mahendra decided to visit his supplier in Kanpur and that once was enough. The smell in the tannery was so foul that he was given sprigs of mint leaves to hold to his nose. Even so he ended the tour rather abruptly.

By now Kanti was called Kantibhai by everyone except his elders. Like his father, he got married early. He was twenty-one. His uncle in Nadiad found a bride for him in their subcaste; a girl who was plucked from school in Surat, before she could complete secondary education, the very day her marriage was fixed. Kanti was a good catch for any parent. The community was proud of the success in faraway Delhi of one their own.

The bride's parents wanted the wedding to take place in their ancestral village and offered to pay for everything. After early years of struggle in Surat, the bride's father had done well in the textile business, and the family were now affluent by local standards. They were generous with the jewellery they gave their daughter, Kokila, at the ceremony; gold of course, but also diamonds and emeralds in a necklace. She was one of two daughters, no son to inherit. Some gossiped that the bride had been chosen keeping this in mind.

Later, Mahendrabhai organized a wedding reception in Delhi and the bride's parents and close relatives came. It was their first trip out of Gujarat. They were put up at the homes of Mahendrabhai's various friends, all vegetarian and Gujaratis, since it was obvious that the villagers would be uncomfortable in a hotel. The best hall in East Delhi was hired for the event.

Three chefs, all Brahmins, came from Surat and were addressed as 'maharaj' by everyone. They were expensive prima donnas. They had travelled by train, insisting on first-class bogeys. They brought their own staff of three who travelled by second-class sleeper. Their baggage included gunny sacks of vegetables peculiar to Gujarati cuisine—purple yams and sorghum beans in their pods. They started preparations two days in advance with assistance from some local hands whose caste backgrounds were checked before they were hired. A separate tent was set up behind the hall for the cooking where no one was allowed to enter except the host family. Under the stern supervision of the three maharajs, generous amounts of garlic were peeled, onions chopped and masalas mixed. A pleasant aroma drifted around the place and permeated the clothing and temporary furnishing.

The pièce de résistance of the meal was undhiyu. The entire dish was cooked in earthen pots sealed and placed upside down in a pit dug in the ground, and steamed over slow-burning fires. In addition to the yam and beans, ripe bananas, small eggplants and fried dumplings made from chickpea flour were thrown in. When the dish arrived on the table steaming hot, oozing oil and smelling of garlic, the Gujarati guests went for it in a big way. The waiters had a hard time keeping the trays loaded as guests dug in, with hot puris and shrikhand on the side.

Everyone ate out of silver-plated thalis that were ordered from Jaipur and had the names of the bride and groom engraved on them along with the date of the wedding. As Mahendrabhai had expected, quite a few of these thalis went missing at the end of the evening, taken away by guests as souvenirs.

Mahendrabhai died young, a year, perhaps more, short of fifty. His parents had not recorded his exact date of birth. He had an undiagnosed heart problem. His doctor had prescribed pills for his high blood pressure, but he never bothered to have them refilled once they ran out. The family waited a day for relatives to arrive from Gujarat before the body was cremated and the ashes taken to Haridwar for immersion in the Ganga.

Mohan, Kantibhai's son—the grandson Mahendrabhai never got to see—was born a year later.

11

Mahendrabhai left the company on a sound footing. The American market had opened up for import of garments from India. Through connections and the greasing of palms, Kantibhai managed to corner more than his share of the quota allocated to the country.

When his output was in excess of his quota Kantibhai would send his products by the truckload to neighbouring Bangladesh. There, a middleman stitched 'Made in Bangladesh' labels on them and shipped them to the United States. But the ruse was exposed a few years later and Kantibhai and his middleman paid a heavy fine. Through interventions at the highest level, no one was sent to prison.

But this was a minor incident and did not affect the business in any way. It continued to grow. Kantibhai made an offer for two plots next to the factory that the owner could not refuse and demolished the shed. A state-of-the-art garment factory came up on the site a year later. It was designed by an American architect who had made Delhi his home. The Uttar Pradesh chief minister came to Noida from Lucknow to inaugurate the new premises after Kantibhai had made a hefty contribution to 'party funds'.

K&M developed a reputation for quality and professional handling of orders, something that was not lost on buyers abroad. The company was soon supplying garments and accessories to upscale shops in New York and London and their branches in other cities. Buyers turned up with their designs and specifications and were wined and dined. Kantibhai was happy to pay for their hotel stays but most of them drew a line at that. Their companies frowned even at this much because it compromised business relationships.

'A buyer from London called me Ken the other day,' Kanti told his wife one evening. 'I liked that.'

Kokilaben smiled.

'I think I will change my name to Ken,' he said. 'It sounds better than Kantibhai, so old-fashioned,'

'Stick to Kantibhai,' his wife said firmly.

That was the end of the discussion.

K&M decided to produce formalwear like shirts and office-going pants to international standards. The government had laid down a condition: fabric could be imported duty free but the products made from this imported fabric could not be sold in India, they must be shipped abroad. This suited companies like K&M fine because the clothes they made could be sold at high prices in the West and the Middle East. But that was not all. The rejects (often just a missing button or a wrinkle in a collar) also brought in money, as they found their way to roadside stalls and hole-in-the-wall shops in popular markets like Sarojini in Delhi and Colaba Causeway in Bombay.

Kantibhai prospered beyond his wildest dreams and the family moved from East Delhi to a mansion built on three acres of land in Chattarpur, South Delhi. Such mansions were called 'farmhouses', but one would have been hard put to find a farmer living in a house so grand. Kantibhai's house had been designed by an architect summoned from Ahmedabad who seemed to have drawn his inspiration from Bollywood sets. There was also a touch, at Kantibhai's request, of the lavish havelis occupied by the cotton-mill owning Seths of Ahmedabad who looked down on upstarts like Kantibhai.

The architect persuaded him to use marble for the exterior instead of bricks, and why not! The architect tried to interest his client in marble from Italy but Kantibhai would not hear of it.

'Desi marble is good enough for me,' he said. 'Haven't you seen the Dilwara Temples in Mount Abu?'

So the two travelled together to the town of Makrana in Rajasthan and returned with huge, unblemished, luminescent pieces.

The marble impressed visitors even before they entered the compound through a large, ornate gold-painted gate almost half a kilometere from the main house. Upon entering, visitors were greeted by a massive fountain in the main hall, twelve feet high. The cascading water was switched on only when there were visitors. The chandelier in blue glass was from Venice, Kantibhai's one allowance to foreign imports. Towards the back were two winding staircases on either side of the hall that lead to the living quarters of the family, five en suite bedrooms and a private family room. Two large paintings, Ravi Varma copies, of scenes from the Ramayana hung in the hall.

A tennis court and swimming pool were added soon afterwards, though neither Kantibhai nor his wife could play the game nor knew how to swim. However, one evening after the servants had retired and the lights switched off, Kokilaben, still clad in her saree, tried out the shallow end of the pool. She liked the experience and would repeat it every now and then.

In the kitchen they had a 'maharaj' of their own, a prima donna from Marwar. The dining table next to the kitchen was massive, made from one piece of green marble that cost a small fortune. His wife wanted something more intimate but Kantibhai wanted to go Bollywood all the way. It could seat twelve. The tableware was thalis, pure silver when the family entertained guests. At other times, at Kokilaben's insistence, it was high-end stainless steel. There was a wash basin next to the kitchen door, since Gujarati food, as the saying goes, tastes better eaten with fingers. Uniformed servants waited on them during lunch and dinner.

Years passed, and Kantibhai's heir, Mohan, grew into his early twenties, finished college in Delhi and then a short management course in USA. Through all this time, K&M was on a roll. The State Trading Corporation had resumed giving the company orders it received from government agencies in Eastern Europe, which was no longer Communist but the new bureaucracy was as efficiently corrupt as the old. These orders still came through a middleman. Kantibhai was generous with kickbacks. At Diwali the middleman told him how many Rolexes he needed for the top level at the ministry and how many boxes of premium Scotch for junior officers. Kantibhai had learnt to trust the man but nevertheless, every once in a while, he made discreet enquiries to find out if the 'gifts' reached the intended recipients.

As business expanded, Kantibhai devised a strategy to sell into both the high-end and budget markets. He divided the company down the middle under two vice presidents.

One took care of orders from their new customers—within India and in other Third World countries—and produced shoddier stuff on the cheap. The other continued with top-of-the-line products for Bloomingdale's, Harrods and some lesser-known outlets on both sides of the Atlantic, where quality was essential.

—

In the summer of 2003, one of K&M's most lucrative clients, a London-based retailer with dozens of outlets worldwide, was having its centenary celebrations. Kantibhai and his wife were sent a personal invitation. He was flattered as well as delighted. Had it included air tickets and hotel accommodation, it would have been icing on the cake. Never mind, of course they would go.

There was more than enough money in the bank and the husband and wife would use the occasion for two weeks of sightseeing in the city. This would be their first trip abroad. Mohan took over. He called their travel agent and told him to book a room at the hotel that was the venue of the celebrations. When the agent called back with room rates of the Dorchester, Kantibhai quickly decided to stay somewhere else. He thought it ridiculous to spend that kind of money for a night's sleep.

The agent found a hotel near Russell Square, a short ride away from Dorchester. It also had the advantage of being close to the upscale clothing shops on Oxford Street and Regent Street. Kokilaben was keen on checking them out. Kantibhai told Mohan to book them economy tickets, but the son talked him out of it.

'Papa, we'll lose face if the host finds out that you have

travelled economy,' he said. 'It is likely that they will send someone with a limo to meet you on arrival. The tags on your luggage will betray you.'

Kantibhai saw the point and reluctantly agreed but the thought briefly crossed his mind to travel first-class one way and economy on return. The tickets cost a small fortune and Kantibhai was not happy until his accountant assured him that they could be put down as company expenses and were tax deductible.

The head of the travel agency arrived to deliver the tickets personally. He brought two small carry-on suitcases, complimentary to first class passengers. Kantibhai had insisted on flying Air India. The food on board would be genuinely vegetarian, no eggs in puddings, and he could just click his fingers if he or his wife needed service. He had been told that you couldn't do that on foreign airplanes.

Since the plane was leaving Delhi late at night, the husband and wife had dinner at home. The seats in first class were wide and comfortable and once the flight attendant reclined them, they slept intermittently all the way. At Heathrow, they found the host had indeed sent a car to pick them up. A Bentley.

They had arrived a day early to get over the jetlag. The hotel was a four-star establishment at a stretch but to Kokilaben's delight it came with a kitchenette that had a stove, a microwave, utensils, plates and other essentials, including a small refrigerator. She'd had the foresight to pack some dry snacks from Haldiram's that would not spoil for weeks, as well as a small dabba of masalas.

The concierge in the lobby pointed the way to a nearby Sainsbury's, a short walk away, where they could shop for groceries. Since they had time on their hands on the first day, they bought tea bags, milk, cornflakes, vegetables and fruit. That evening they made a meal out of the fruits, amazed by their quality. They had seen nothing like them back home, clean, freshly picked and oozing with juice. Kokilaben was particularly taken by the cherries and peaches. She decided she would be quite content living off the fruits during their stay, her husband could have the Haldiram's stuff, bread or toast with a spread of mango pickles. Mohan had told them that London was now almost half Indian, and there were scores of restaurants where they would find good vegetarian food, including Gujarati fare. But neither parent thought it wise to spend too much on food. Besides, they had heard that Pakistanis and Bangladeshis ran many of these restaurants. They would rather starve than risk eating food cooked by a cow-eating Muslim.

At six-thirty sharp the next evening, a car arrived at the hotel door and the concierge told them to come down. Kantibhai was in a bespoke bandhgala, Kokilaben looked splendid in her Kanjeevaram silk saree.

'You look lovely, Madam,' the uniformed chauffeur told her as he opened the door for them.

'Thank you,' she said shyly, two of the dozen odd English words she knew.

This impressed her husband.

At the entrance to the ballroom at the Dorchester they were personally greeted by the company's chairman, a hereditary knight of the realm. They had not met before but Sir Harold Sedley had been well briefed by his staff. He greeted them with folded hands and a namaste. He asked some reassuringly personal questions—about their son, their flight—and Kantibhai was pleased.

After cocktails, fresh juices for Kantibhai and Kokilaben,

they were seated on a round table of eight close to the head table. Someone had had the foresight to seat an Indian couple next to them to put them at ease. He was one of their senior executives in Leicester who spoke fluent Hindi and, being from Leicester, understood Gujarati. The other Indian couple were Tamil Brahmins and vegetarian. In ordinary circumstances the company would not have invited them to something this grand.

The waiter assigned to their table noticed that Kokilaben was munching on the bread and had not touched the camembert soufflé on her plate. He understood, being an experienced waiter who had served people from all parts of the world, that she was afraid the soufflé might have eggs in it. He went to the kitchen and came back with a plate of sliced fruit. The plate of fresh fruit quietly placed in front of her brought a smile to Kokilaben's lips.

'Thank you,' she said with a shy smile.

Kantibhai and the Tamil couple had no problem with the vegetarian menu especially designed for the table. The two white couples on the table were polite. In the beginning they made an attempt at conversation but once food was served, they kept to themselves.

While pudding was served, there were speeches but they were mercifully short. Kantibhai and Kokilaben endured a string quartet playing classical selections. They were back in their hotel rooms before ten.

The next day they took the Jubilee Line train in the morning to Neasden station to visit what was allegedly the largest Hindu temple outside India. It belonged to a religious sect that was entirely Gujarati and that was why it was in Wembley. They sat cross-legged on the marble floor during kirtan, Kantibhai with the men and his wife with the women.

Afterwards, they walked around the neighbourhood and, assured by fellow Gujaratis they met in the temple, went to a desi restaurant that served a decent thali, theplas with shrikand and dhoklas. Kantibhai dug in but Kokilaben just nibbled, impatient to get back to the fruits in her hotel fridge. They walked down to Alperton tube station to pick up souvenirs for their domestic staff back home. The shops were owned by local Indians and Kantibhai was tempted to bargain but then thought better of it. They settled on some battery-operated ladies and men's watches.

It was an altogether satisfactory trip, and one that made Kantibhai feel confident about the future of the company. The reception he and Kokilaben received at the clients' centenary dinner was ample proof of how much their products were valued. It was time to groom young Mohan, so that he could take over when the time was right.

Shortly after his return from London, Kantibhai took on the designation of chairman of K&M, while Mohan was made president.

12

In the smooth and narrow stream of Kantibhai's life there had been a little disturbance once. Not quite a whirlpool, but an eddy. It is a side story that need not be written, for in the end it had no bearing on his personal and professional life. But every experience leaves its mark, however small, so let it be told.

Shortly after K&M set up that new, state-of-the-art garment factory in Noida, the company hired Radhika Ram. By this time Kantibhai's garment business had greatly expanded. Although Kanti was fussy about each new recruit, Radhika had been recommended by a minister, so he had no choice but to take her. This minister, incidentally, had nothing to do with textiles or exports; he was in charge of information and broadcasting but, more importantly, he held cabinet rank. A minister was a minister, thought Kantibhai, someday he may prove useful.

Radhika was from Orissa, like the minister. She ended up at K&M because there was a time when the minister was more than friendly with her mother. He first met the lady at one of his public durbars when she was already married and a mother, and he already a minister in the Central Government, and he was smitten. She had been part of a delegation of residents who wanted the minister to sanction a public bus service to their locality. When a message was delivered that the minister wanted her to discuss the matter with him in private one evening, she went willingly. She enjoyed the attention of an important man.

Though no longer so young, she was still a beauty. She was tall and statuesque and heads turned when she was in the street, out on errands or shopping. The only thing that had prevented her finding a prosperous husband had been her caste and the fact that she was illiterate.

The minister arranged a post for her husband in the local administration in Bhubaneshwar, which came with modest government quarters. The post was clerical and did not pay well, so the minister supplemented it with a monthly stipend in cash.

The minister's work kept him mostly in Delhi, but when he was in his constituency, he visited Radhika's house and sometimes spent the night in the spare bedroom with the mother. If the husband had any problem with the arrangement, the minister was not aware of it. Whatever fights they had was not his business.

The two children, Radhika and her younger brother, got used to it after some time, despite the gossip and snide remarks in school. They even began to look forward to the minister's visits. He always came bearing gifts for them, imported chocolates, tins of biscuits and other such stuff that was not available in the provincial backwater.

Like her mother before her, Radhika was sixteen when, despite her protests, a marriage was arranged for her to a boy two years older than her. She had matriculated and yearned to have a college education. But the boy was an attractive catch for her parents and they had their way. His family were farmers with a herd of cattle and several hectares of land where they grew rice and cattle feed.

The in-laws were kind people but Radhika was miserable living in a joint family and outside the city. One day, without telling anyone, she packed her bag and returned to her parents' place. Her parents lost face, as did the boy's parents. There was no divorce that anyone knew of, but it wasn't necessary as neither Radhika nor the husband were thinking of remarrying yet.

Radhika's grades were not spectacular, but she was still keen to go to college and hopefully move out to a big city. One evening, when the minister was visiting, Radhika pleaded her case with him. Her parents too were keen for her to move away now that she had brought disgrace to the family.

'I will see what I can do,' the minister said, as she sat on the floor in the living room, massaging his legs, perhaps a little too sensually. The parents looked on.

When the minister returned to Delhi, he made a few calls and despite her poor grades Radhika was admitted to Miranda House through the Scheduled Caste quota. A women's only college of Delhi University, Miranda House was where many of the brightest, most fashionable girls from largely privileged North Indian families had been coming to study since it was founded in 1948. Lady Edwina Mountbatten had laid the foundation stone.

Radhika was allocated a shared room in the college hostel. The minister paid her fees, and gave her a generous monthly allowance. It was all done through his staff. He lay down one rule, though: she was to visit him only at his office and not at his residence. He gave her a number to call, not his own, if she needed to get in touch with him after office hours. His wife was aware of the existence of his mistress and her family—Bhubaneswar, with a population of less than a million, was, after all, a small town. She was not a happy woman, although she had reconciled herself to his extramarital affairs, and there would be more trouble for him if she found out that the daughter of his mistress had moved to the capital and was under his wing.

It wasn't love for wife and family or a desire for domestic harmony that explained the minister's wish for discretion. The reason was that he owed his ministerial post to his wife's family. They were among the largest producers of iron ore in Odisha. They won the rights through a manipulated government auction, which was a blatant land-grab, a bonanza for them but disaster for the Adivasis, the indigenous tribes, whose forest lands were taken away from them. The Adivasis had been in possession for centuries but had no papers to prove ownership. The government had promised resettlement for those who were displaced by mining projects, but nothing had come of it. Meanwhile, families like the minister's in-laws had amassed great wealth and power—enough to influence both the state and central governments.

Radhika's roommate at Miranda was Pratibha, a Punjabi girl from Kenya. The choice of a foreign student had been deliberate. The warden was aware that many of the local students would not want to share the room with Radhika—she had found admission through the reserved category, so it was common knowledge that she was Dalit. Pratibha had no problem with that. Her grandfather had gone to East Africa as an indentured labourer to lay down the tracks for the railway there. Caste had ceased to matter to her family two generations ago.

After some initial misery, Radhika adjusted to the new surroundings quite well. Her roommate had a lot to do with this. Pratibha was shy, a person of few words, but friendly.

Unlike the local girls, the girl from Nairobi was not in the habit of prying into the personal lives of people. The two got on well. In the beginning, Pratibha tried to converse in English but turned to Hindi when she realized that Radhika was more comfortable with it. Most afternoons and evenings, the two hung out in the college and sometimes went for a stroll around the university campus. They were expected to be behind the college gates by seven, unless a pass was given to stay out late for some reason. Their favourite café was Nirula's, the restaurant chain that had opened a branch opposite the University Faculty of Arts, where they ordered cold coffee and cheese sandwiches; a more grown-up and sophisticated thing, in their estimation, than tea and samosas. Both envied the girls who had local guardians on the college register whom they were allowed to visit on weekends.

Some Sunday afternoons, at Pratibha's suggestion, they would go to catch a Hollywood movie at one of the cinemas in Connaught Place—Rivoli, Regal, Odeon, and Plaza, their favourite. The first time, they bought tickets for the cheaper seats, and were uncomfortable the entire ninety minutes because of the stares they received from men who were not used to seeing women unaccompanied in the front stalls. After that, they bought the more expensive seats at the back.

When they went in a group with other hostel girls to the afternoon screening, they had coffee and sandwiches at one of the posh restaurants and returned before curfew. Only once did the girls reach late, and they were lucky the warden let them off with a warning. She was not one to take such transgressions lightly.

Delhi University was still Punjabi-conservative in those days. Salwar kameez was the norm; rarely did one see women in jeans or slacks, and most of these were Miranda House girls. Radhika wanted to dress like them. Freed from her small-town milieu, she wanted a new life.

'I need to buy some clothes,' she said to her roommate. 'Would you mind coming to CP with me?'

Pratibha jumped at the opportunity. The truth was that Radhika wanted her friend's advice on what to buy.

They took the bus to Connaught Place and splurged, making substantial dents in their allowances. They ignored the sarees and salwar-kameez sets, of which they both had plenty in their college closets. They took their time, going from shop to shop, and returned with bags full of functional but attractive cotton clothes, lipsticks, bras, and shoes. Now they were Delhi girls, more or less.

The university had special classes in spoken English for students like Radhika whose earlier education had been mostly in vernacular languages. Attendance in these classes was not compulsory, but students who felt the need were encouraged to take them.

Since the classes were open to everyone, it was a good way for boys and girls from different colleges to meet. These one-hour classes were held twice a week in the afternoon in the Faculty of Arts building after the regular teaching was over. There was no fee, but students had to enroll and attend regularly.

The lecturer who was assigned to these classes had freshly arrived from Cambridge, having chosen to return to her home country rather than settle down in Britain. She could not adjust to life without servants. The daughter of a senior bureaucrat, joint secretary to the government of

India, Neeta Behl was only a little older than her students but had far greater confidence. She belonged to a different, classier world. Radhika wished she could be half as elegant and sophisticated as her.

In the first two sessions, Radhika did not say a word; she just took notes and sometimes pretended to, in order to avoid eye contact with the teacher. After listening to other students having a go at spoken English, she started raising questions with Neeta's encouragement. This was not so difficult after all, even fun, she thought to herself.

Soon Neeta started giving the students homework over the weekend—extracts to read from Jane Austen's *Pride and Prejudice* and Thomas Hardy's *Far from the Madding Crowd*, to be discussed in class the following week. She distributed copies of the novels to be returned afterwards. A number of students bought their own paperbacks from a bookshop in Kashmiri Gate, a short bus ride away, so that they could mark and underline passages. Radhika also bought Hindi translations, which helped her enormously in participating in the discussions.

She may not have been the brightest of students, but she was a determined one. She burned the midnight oil and managed to pass the Bachelor's degree. She was denied an 'honours' degree but was happy to have passed.

Her parents were delighted to have a graduate in the family but were deeply upset when she told them that she would be making Delhi her home. They were hurt that they had not been consulted on their daughter's decision; she had presented it to them as a fait accompli. In three years, the girl from Orissa had transformed herself into a Delhi girl.

But she had to find employment if she was to survive in Delhi. Radhika was determined not to rely on financial help from her generous benefactor once she finished college. She had not seen him for the past three years. Her instruction had been to not meet or call him, and she had stuck to it.

She scanned the weekend newspapers, and after an interview, she found a sales position at a small department store in South Extension that did not require any expertise. It did not take her long to figure out that it was her looks and statuesque figure that were responsible for landing her a job at the front counter.

It was a long commute from Kamla Nagar, where she had been staying as a paying guest with a family since she graduated. Being close to the campus, it was a neighbourhood she had grown accustomed to, it was her comfort zone. She shared the room with a student from the Northeast who kept to herself. Pratibha had returned to Nairobi.

After a few weeks and through enquiries, Radhika found accommodation in Kotla, closer to work, in one of the back streets. It was a fifteen-minute walk from her workplace. Four women, more or less of the same age, shared a two-bedroom flat above that of their landlady. The lease was in the name of one of the women who had allotted the larger bedroom to herself and her friend. The rent was split four ways and was within Radhika's budget.

The tiny kitchen was shared by all four. The ancient fridge was kept stocked, and at the end of each month, they split the household expenses. Anyone could volunteer to cook the evening meal, but more often than not, they ordered from a nearby dhaba that made home deliveries. They had a phone in the house, but one could not call long distance on it. The girls walked to an STD/PCO booth outside a shop if they wished to call home. These STD calls were metered, and one paid immediately after the call.

International calls were also possible from there, but the need for that never arose except once, when Radhika dialled Nairobi. Her friend from college was getting married to a London-returned Punjabi boy. She had sent her college roommate a personalized invitation. It had been over a year since they had parted, and Radhika was touched by the gesture. They did not hear from each other again.

The two bedrooms of the Kotla flat were Spartan; the curtains were thin sheets that let the light in at dawn, and the cotton mattresses were so thin that the body could feel the wood of the bed below. Two of the more enterprising residents bought sheets of foam to cover the mattresses to soften them. At the insistence of the forever prying landlady, the flat was off-limits to male visitors, but exceptions were made for relatives who could be entertained in the shared living room.

It was around this time that Radhika had her first serious boyfriend, Virendra Kaul, a graduate from St Stephen's whom she had met once briefly while in college. He had been in his final year while she was in her second. She must have created an impression because he tracked her down to the shop where she was working. He was tall, like her, and handsome. He was always smartly dressed, which impressed Radhika.

Virendra held an executive position at a foreign bank, the perks of which included a rent-free flat in Jor Bagh, the upscale South Delhi colony, plus a brand new Maruti car. He entered the store in South Extension on the pretext of buying some shirts and expressed surprise when he saw Radhika there. She helped him select some button-downs in solid whites and blues. While she was preparing the bill, he asked her if they could meet again.

'I would love to,' she told him and quietly wrote down her number on the back of his bill.

The following week, they went for the six o'clock movie at Plaza, followed by dinner at Gaylords around the corner. She was overwhelmed by the uniformed service, the spotless white tablecloth, and the ambient lighting. When her napkin fell off her lap, the waiter promptly replaced it with a fresh one.

She knew, more or less, how to handle the cutlery in front of her, but the listing on the heavy menu was a mystery to her. 'Let me order for both of us,' he said.

That was fine with her.

It was one of the fanciest restaurants in town, and he had come with the intention of eating something from the 'Continental' section of the menu. But he changed his mind and ordered rogan josh, raita and daal, to be accompanied with naans and rice. Radhika felt comfortable when he tore the fluffy naan with his fingers and scooped up the curry.

It was the best meal she had had since arriving in Delhi and in the poshest restaurant. Afterwards, he dropped her home, but around the corner, within walking distance from her place. She insisted on it, wishing to avoid idle gossip among her flatmates and the neighbours.

After several such outings he invited her for dinner in his flat. Following some awkward attempts at kissing they moved to his bedroom where he unbuttoned her blouse. She unwrapped the sari and asked him to switch off the lights before she took off the rest. As he kissed her firm breasts, Radhika almost swooned. She had not made love since she left her husband. To her disappointment, Virendra came quickly. She guessed rightly that he was a novice in such matters, perhaps a virgin. She did not let on that she was not.

Virendra was from Kashmir, a Pandit by caste, sharp-featured and fair complexioned and like most people of his community, as proud of these physical attributes as of his superior education. By now, he was head over heels in love with the dusky beauty from Orissa. He phoned her at the store every day and met her often after work. His performance in bed improved.

The shop where Radhika worked was open till eight in the evening, six days a week. But the sales staff took turns leaving at five twice a week. On Mondays, the day the shop was closed, she spent time at Virendra's flat while he was at work. The servant was instructed to let her in and made a light meal for her at lunchtime, usually a sandwich or an omelette loaded with cheese, tomatoes, onions and a touch of freshly chopped chilies. The spacious, well-appointed flat made for a nice, relaxed change from her own shared space.

There were times when she spent the night with Virendra. Her flatmates didn't ask where she had been, and she didn't offer explanations. It was an unwritten rule among the four women. They were all in search of partners and steady boyfriends. Most times, Radhika took an auto-rickshaw, a short distance away to Jor Bagh from the shop on Ring Road and her flat in Kotla. He dropped her home afterward in his car or ordered a taxi for which he paid the driver in advance.

Virendra Kaul came from a distinguished family. An uncle of his had been an ambassador in Moscow, and another had been a governor of Maharashtra. He had studied at Oxford on a Rhodes scholarship, and his parents had hoped he would join the Indian Administrative Service, but Virendra had decided there was more money to be made in banking. The idea of driving around in the back of an Ambassador car as a babu did not find favour with him.

Certainly, the perks offered by the bank were better.

His mother urged him to marry and settle down. After a few months, he thought he would tell his mother about Radhika. Being a practical man, conscious of his status and pedigree, he made some discreet inquiries about Radhika with the intention of proposing marriage. His parents preferred him to marry within their community, a fellow Kashmiri Brahmin, but they could be persuaded. They were proud to consider themselves liberal in such matters.

But when a well-connected colleague from Orissa, alerted by Radhika's surname, told him of her background—that she was from a Dalit family and it was widely known that her mother had been the mistress of a well-known politician—Virendra dropped her overnight. His family might be liberal, but not that liberal. Radhika called him after she had not heard from him for several days. Virendra made excuses for not meeting and promised to call back.

But she never heard from him again. Radhika was devastated by the callous way he had dumped her. She had expectations and thought the relationship would be taken to its logical conclusion. But she was no fool; deep down, she had an inkling of why he had suddenly withdrawn like that. Still, she wished he had the grace to meet her face to face before parting. She shed more than a few tears the night she finally accepted the truth.

After six months as a salesperson, Radhika realized she was in a dead-end job. Her flatmates led more interesting lives. One of them was a reporter at a national paper, and the one from the Northeast was a maître d' at a posh restaurant.

They all got on well and sometimes stepped out together to take in a movie at Chanakya and eat afterward in some restaurant nearby, if their working hours permitted. By then, she had moved from Indian dishes to pizzas, pastas, and burgers. She put up a happy face but was bored and often lonely. She wanted to move on in life.

One day, with great reluctance and hesitation, she called her initial benefactor directly at his office.

'Hello Uncle,' she said with all the deference she could muster. 'How are you?' Over the years, she had come to despise him, as one does those whose favours one would rather not have but can't do without.

The 'uncle' was no fool. He guessed the girl needed something, but he went along with it.

'I hear you have finished college. Congratulations,' the minister said. 'How are your parents?'

'They are fine, Uncle,' she replied. She had not seen them in two years, and he was aware of that. Still, there was no sarcasm in his voice. These things happened; people moved on.

They made some small talk before he got to the point.

'Is there anything I can do?' he asked.

Radhika told him where she was working and that she was looking for something more interesting to do. The fact that this was the first time she had called in the four years she had been in the city worked in her favour. He had stopped visiting her mother by then and had moved on to a younger woman. The minister made a few inquiries after she called off.

The next day, Kantibhai's office called her.

Since she was recommended by the minister, who had been minister of state for textiles in Mahendrabhai's time, Kantibhai decided to interview Radhika himself. On the appointed day, when she walked in, his heart skipped a beat. She looked striking in an understated silk saree that she carried with elegance and grace, and yet there was something earthy and sensual about her. Tall and dusky, with not the slightest trace of diffidence, she was the exact opposite of the women of his community, none of whom, including his wife, had truly excited him.

He had intended to place her in one of the clerical positions. He changed his mind and placed her in the public relations and hospitality section he intended to set up. It was to be a small operation, just one person, who would share a secretary with one of the executives. He also decided to place her on his floor and under his direct supervision.

He asked Radhika a few standard questions: her education, marital status, and the salary she expected. She told him she was single, which was technically true. As for salary, she left it to Kantibhai, whatever he considered appropriate. From the intensity of his gaze when he spoke to her, she could tell that she had made an impression on him. She was used to the attention of men and was not averse to his. He was, after all, the owner of the company. He also looked reassuringly mature, older than his years. She guessed he was thirty or less, but in his bearing, very much the boss. Physically, he wasn't quite her type, but she wasn't looking to share his bed. She only wanted to please him as an efficient employee and work her way up to a good position and salary.

Kanti gave her a brief job description. She was to meet visitors from abroad at the airport and look after their needs during their stay: hotel accommodation, taking them sightseeing if they were so inclined, entertaining them at fancy restaurants, and so on. If they wanted to eat like the locals, he instructed her to take them to Moti Mahal or Karim's, but to ensure that they didn't eat too much and get the Delhi belly! She was to be at their beck and call twenty-four/seven, but there would be no overtime. Radhika had no problem with any of it. The salary was several notches higher than what she was paid at the department store.

Through connections and greasing of palms, the company had been given a pass for the newly inaugurated Indira Gandhi International Airport that allowed a designated employee to meet new arrivals in the baggage area after they cleared the immigration formalities. The pass could not be transferred.

This was a privilege that the airport authorities normally extended to diplomatic missions and select government offices. Kantibhai had also requested access to the VIP lounge at the airport for his arriving and departing buyers, but this had been denied. He had been pushing his luck.

A month after Radhika's employment, an important buyer from London sent word that he was arriving in Delhi. Could a meeting be set up? Yes, of course, K&M replied promptly. The company had not done business with Harrods, a famous luxury store, before. Apparently, the department store had been unhappy with its current supplier of casuals in India, who had become greedy, and they were looking for other possibilities. The Harrods' management had zoomed in on Kantibhai's factory.

This was Radhika's baptism by fire. The plane landed after midnight, as they all seemed to do. Kantibhai had sent his personal driver with the Mercedes to pick her up and take her to the airport to receive the client. Kanti had thought of going personally, but his manager had talked him out of it.

'Let us not seem too keen, sir,' he had advised his boss.

Before leaving, Radhika had checked with British Airways that the flight was on time. She had given herself ample time to reach before the flight landed. This was her first visit to the airport, and it would be her first face-to-face meeting with a foreign client.

Her pass, with her photo identification, allowed her into the terminal. She had almost an hour to kill. She sat in a chair and brushed off the mosquitoes. Next time, she would plan better. The office had printed out a foot-long card with the visitor's name in large letters: 'Mr Needham'.

As a first-class passenger, Needham was among the first to clear immigration formalities.

'Welcome to Delhi, sir,' Radhika greeted him with a smile when the lanky middle-aged man in a smart black suit saw his name and walked up to her. If Radhika was nervous, she did not show it.

He extended his hand. 'It is very kind of you to come to receive me so late in the evening,' he had pleasantly.

'It is my pleasure, sir.'

She had located his Louis Vuitton suitcase on the carousel and put it on the trolley with help from an airline employee. When she tried to push it, Needham did not let her.

'Please let me do that,' he said as he took the trolley from her. She worried that she might be ticked off if the office found out.

When the customs officials saw her pass, they nodded the two through.

As instructed, on the way back in the Mercedes, she sat up front with the driver.

After Needham's suite had been assigned at the hotel and the formalities were over, the driver dropped her home.

At ten in the morning, Radhika picked Needham up from his hotel and dropped him at the factory, where Kantibhai took over. She came to the hotel at seven in the evening to take Needham to Kantibhai's residence for dinner. The visitor uttered one word when the gates of the farmhouse opened and he set eyes on the lit-up mansion: 'Wow!'

The tables had been laid on the lawns instead of indoors, as the menu was not vegetarian. This was official business, and exceptions had to be made. Kokilaben had confined herself to her bedroom. A five-star hotel was doing the catering. A sitar and tabla player provided soft music from some distance. There was a pleasant breeze, the first hint of the impending winter.

Some of the key senior staff had been invited with their wives, but they had come alone with excuses for the absence of their spouses. It was assumed by the host that the spouses would have had to struggle with using forks and knives and that small talk would have been alien to them.

Radhika was not on the guest list. She waited in the car with the driver, and someone from the catering staff brought them plates laden with food, some paper napkins and bottled water. She had been about to get in the back seat of the car with her plate, but the driver suggested otherwise.

'Didi, let's not eat in the car. The firangis have sensitive noses. The car will smell of spices and garlic,' he said.

They placed their plates on the hood of the car and ate standing. She was on a diet and passed some of the food onto the driver's plate. He made only a half-hearted effort to stop her. This was a treat for him.

They began to chat, the first time they had had any kind of conversation. She asked about his family. He told her he was from Bihar and had a college degree. After his marriage, he had left his bride with his parents and come to Delhi in search of a clerical job. After months of looking everywhere and getting nothing, he had taken driving lessons at the suggestion of a friend. He had landed the job as one of the drivers in Kantibhai's factory. The smattering of English he knew had helped.

'This is my fourth year with the company,' he told her. 'The salary is good. Unlike their family driver, I'm on the company's payroll, which entitles me to overtime pay and other benefits like three weeks of annual leave. That is when I visit my family back in my village.'

'Why don't you bring your family here?' she asked.

'I will someday. Right now, I need my wife in the village to look after my aging mother,' he replied. 'I'm the only son.'

It had been largely a one-sided conversation. Radhika had revealed little about herself. She had realized that as far as backgrounds went, they had a lot in common and she didn't want him to know that.

It was Needham's first visit to Delhi. He was a senior executive at Harrods, not a buyer, though the buyers that worked in the Asian market reported to him. He was impressed by the way K&M was managed, though he thought the lavish dinner at Kantibhai's residence was a bit over the top.

The next day, after he had had a light lunch at the hotel, Radhika arrived to take him sightseeing. This time she was obliged to sit in the back next to him, with the guide next to the driver. They made the usual rounds: Humayun's Tomb, a few minutes from the hotel, the Red Fort, and Qutub Minar further out. The visitor did not get off at any of these points; perhaps the beggars tapping on the window every time the car stopped had put him off.

Since there was time to kill, they drove around Connaught Place and the Rashtrapati Bhavan area. When they returned to the hotel, Needham insisted on tipping the guide, over Radhika's protestations, an amount that astonished her. Then he went to his room to shower and change from his sweaty clothes while Radhika waited in the lobby. He came down without his jacket, refreshed.

Kantibhai had arranged for Radhika to take him out for dinner. He had wanted to visit an authentic Indian restaurant, nothing fancy. The office, from previous experience, had seen that coming. They had suggested she take him to Moti Mahal in Daryaganj.

When she opened the front door of the car, he insisted she sit at the back. At the restaurant, Needham asked the driver and Radhika to join him at the table. The driver made the usual excuse that the expensive car would not be safe left unattended. The office had assured Radhika that they would have no problem with her joining him at dinner if he invited her, so she did.

He asked her to order for both of them.

'Don't worry, I'm used to spicy food. Chicken tikka masala is Britain's national dish,' he said with a chuckle. 'Order what you think is best here.'

Radhika felt relaxed in his company now. She placed the order: the house specialty, tandoori chicken with makhani daal and naan.

The loud live music outdoors prevented much conversation, and she was grateful for that. The evening went off well. She had had some trouble following his English accent, but he had put her at ease.

When they came out, she expected him to be dropped back at the hotel. But his next request floored her.

'I want to see the red-light district,' he said suddenly. 'I've heard a lot about it.'

The man had probably confused Delhi's red-light area for Bombay's Kamathipura and its infamous cages, Radhika thought. She hadn't a clue where to take him. She caught the driver's eye in the rearview mirror.

'Didi, leave it to me,' he said to her in Hindi.

The driver decided to take the scenic route. This time of night, Chandni Chowk would not be crowded. He headed toward the Red Fort to enter through the eastern end of the chowk. The shops were shuttered, and the car glided through the arterial road with ease.

Garstin Bastion Road was named after a British officer of the East India Company and was changed to Swami Shradhanand Marg two decades after Independence. Both the old and the new name were a mouthful. So everyone simply called it G.B. Road.

The road ran between two famous gates of the old city, Lahori Gate that, in old times, probably connected Delhi to Lahore, and Ajmeri Gate, that led to the Holy City of Ajmer in the south. There were dozens of brothels on several floors but none of them on the ground floor, where retail shops operated during the day. Customers came here from far for automobile parts, hardware and machinery.

Needham had read about the place. The brothels had existed from Mughal times. The 'kothas' were rather shabby, the going rates for the prostitutes were reasonable. G.B. Road was largely the haunt of students and daily wage earners with wives in the villages. The girls were checked for disease on a regular basis but only the foolhardy would rely on them. Prostitution was a criminal offence in Delhi but authorities turned a blind eye to activities on this particular stretch, because it served a need.

Needham had no wish to have any sex here—or indeed, anywhere. It had never interested him and he had been branded a freak by his friends once they had assured themselves that he wasn't a homosexual. But he was fascinated by those who did have sex, especially what was considered illicit or deviant sex. But he never entered brothels and sex clubs and bars. He only liked to walk around in red light areas.

He asked the driver to stop somewhere for a while. The Mercedes came to a halt opposite a non-descript building. The red lights at the entrance to the staircase indicated that there was a brothel above. Needham said he would take a walk, but the driver advised him, with some help from Radhika, that he stay in the car. Otherwise, he would be surrounded by pimps. He had already taken the precaution of locking all four doors of the car.

Needham looked disappointed but laughed and said, 'Ah well. The Lord keeps me from sin and VD.'

Radhika blushed.

'I'm so sorry,' Needham said. 'How stupid of me. You must excuse me, that was most improper.'

'Please do not apologize. I found it funny. We appreciate humour in India,' she said, impressed by her English. Perhaps her nervousness had suddenly improved her vocabulary, she said to herself and laughed a little. Needham interpreted the laugh as her maturity and good nature.

'Thank you for being a sport,' he said.

The car moved on. Radhika considered the evening a success.

She waited in the lobby of the hotel while Needham went to change into a suit and bring his bags down. At the airport, he tipped the driver handsomely and handed

Radhika a paper bag. She opened it on the way home. It was a box of chocolates from Harrods with the Royal Crest on it. The bag also contained a handwritten thank you note on the hotel's stationery that mentioned that the thin mint chocolates were the Queen's favourite.

Three months later, K&M landed the Harrods account. Kantibhai was pleased with the way Radhika had handled the visitor. She was mentioned in a thank you note Needham had sent soon after his departure.

Visitors from abroad, however, were few and far between, so Radhika's duties at the company were expanded. She was to assist Mrs Swati Malhotra, Kantibhai's trusted and discreet secretary of long standing. Radhika was to run errands, take phone calls for Kantibhai whenever required, and follow up on his appointments. A small salary raise came with these assignments. Radhika was happy.

Some months later, when an important American buyer was returning, Kantibhai went to the hotel to see her off. She ran a wholesale business out of New York, and her orders were large and lucrative. After the bags were loaded, Radhika opened the front door of the Mercedes to accompany her to the airport.

'There is no need for that. It is getting late. You go home, dear, have a good rest. I've been in and out of your airport many times,' the visitor said kindly.

Radhika looked at Kantibhai standing near her for guidance. He nodded to indicate that it was fine.

'I'll take a taxi home,' she told her employer when the office car left for the airport with the visitor, 'but first I should go back and check the room to see that nothing has been left behind.'

She still had the keys, and she headed for the hotel elevator. Kantibhai followed her.

'I will drop you home in my car,' he said and got in the elevator with her.

In the room, Radhika took a quick look in the bathroom and cupboards. When she bent down to go through the drawers, she sensed Kanti's eyes on her back. She made the search of the room a little longer than necessary.

On the way out, she opened the door for her employer, standing quite close to him. Kanti closed it and tried to kiss her on the mouth. She turned in time, and the kiss was planted on her cheek. No words were exchanged, and Radhika showed no emotion. In the car, she sat next to the driver as expected and politely said goodbye to her employer when she got off, as if nothing had happened.

The next encounter was engineered by Kanti in a similar situation. This time she let him kiss her on the lips in the vacated hotel room. When he tried to squeeze her breasts, she quickly withdrew.

'Sir, please,' she said and turned away to adjust her saree.

A couple of weeks later, in another hotel room, she let his tongue inside her mouth. He had always wanted to do that but had never tried it with Kokila. Now, when he pushed his tongue clumsily into her mouth, Radhika pretended inexperience. He pressed her against the wall, unbuttoned her blouse and lifted the bra to kiss her breasts. She could feel his penis rubbing against her. She decided this much was enough, she would make him wait just a little longer.

'Please sir, please,' she said and pulled away.

By now Kantibhai's personal driver had his suspicions. Three personal hotel visits to see off a guest with his young secretary was unusual. But his lips would remain sealed. He would not gossip, it wasn't worth losing his job.

After the next visitor, a Dutch lady, left for the airport,

boss and secretary returned to her room and used the bed that still smelt of the departed guest's perfume. Kanti came in minutes. Radhika faked it.

Back in the office, Kantibhai felt the situation had become untenable. He had difficulty keeping his eyes off her. He was no fool and realized that sooner or later the staff would sense something was going on between the two. While that worried him, he could brazen it out, but he was petrified of gossip trickling to his wife, whom, despite evidence to the contrary, he loved dearly. She had given him a son.

A week later, when his senior secretary was away from her desk, he called Radhika in. He suggested that she put in her papers and assured her that he would take care of her. Unlike her employer, Radhika was already aware that there was malicious gossip about her circulating in the factory.

'Why are you resigning?' the personnel manager asked, avoiding a smirk. 'We are happy with your performance, and you've only been with us four months.'

'Sir,' she said politely, 'I find the commute to Noida difficult. I have to change two buses on the way.'

'Have you found another job?'

'Yes,' she replied.

He left it at that.

Mrs Malhotra, the senior secretary, arranged a small farewell party in the cafeteria's private dining room for senior staff. She had invited Kantibhai, but he had excused himself, saying his presence would make the staff uncomfortable. He was right about that.

Mrs Malhotra then decided to make it a ladies-only

event. At Kantibhai's suggestion, she presented Radhika with a bouquet on behalf of the company. Her tenure had been quite short; anything more than a bouquet would have raised eyebrows.

Kantibhai bought Radhika a three-bedroom DDA flat just off Khel Gaon Marg in South Delhi, built barely five years earlier, ahead of the Asian Games that Delhi had hosted. It was a relatively new walk-up on the second floor, but it was spacious and overlooked a small park at the back. Hers was the smallest block and parking in the narrow lane leading to it might have created problems, but that was fine. She didn't have a car and had not yet learned to drive. She loved the flat.

Her benefactor paid for the furnishings—living room furniture, kitchen equipment, curtains, a fair-sized television, a large fridge and two air-conditioners. She arranged for a plumber to convert the squatting toilet into a Western one. The masons took their time breaking down a wall to join two bedrooms to make one large one. She gave the workers a hard time on specifications and dangled a bonus if they completed the work ahead of schedule.

Kantibhai was a bit taken aback by these expenditures, much more than he expected, but did not say anything. Everything was paid in cash. He had plenty of that in several bank safe deposit boxes. Radhika moved in as soon as the place was ready for occupation, after saying teary farewells to her roommates at the Kotla flat, not far from her new home.

Meanwhile, Kanti set her up in business. Through his now wide connections, he got her an agency for supplying gas cylinders for cooking. It was a government-run operation under the Ministry of Petroleum and Natural Gas, conceived by a socialist government some decades ago to replace kerosene stoves and wood-burning chullahs in Indian homes. These subsidized gas cylinders were distributed by hundreds of agencies across the country. Radhika became the owner of one such agency.

She found storage room in an area where rents were low and not far from her residence. She needed only two employees: one to guard the cylinders and take orders by phone, and the other to make deliveries on a bicycle. Delivering was a back-breaking job. In many places, the delivery man had to carry the gas cylinders up several flights of steps. Bringing down the empty ones was somewhat easier. Some of the more affluent customers lived in high rises with lifts, but the delivery boy was not allowed to use them. He soon learned that the poorer customers often tipped more, and some kind kitchen employees packed him leftover food.

Both guard and delivery man were paid a pittance, less than minimum wage. Their earnings came from tips, and they were allowed to use the back section of the storage room as their living quarters. They slept on a mattress on the floor and used a communal toilet facility nearby.

All the deliveries were in the neighbourhood, to dedicated customers. There was no shortage of them; cylinders were hard to come by, and there was a long waiting list. Part of Radhika's income came from giving the cylinders out of turn to the desperate for a charge. This was illegal, and she would lose the agency if she were caught. But Kanti would make sure she wasn't.

It was practically a self-running business; all Radhika had to do was keep accounts and update the list of customers.

She earned more than twice what K&M had paid her. Every few days, she would visit the storeroom to collect the sales proceeds and go through the accounts. It was a cash-only business, which had tax advantages. Her visits to the storeroom were always unannounced, keeping the staff on their toes.

Kantibhai's visits to the flat were always discreet. Only his trusted driver was in the know, which could not be avoided. Kanti dropped by in the evening on his way home. It was a little out of the way, but his wife was used to him arriving late from work. He never stayed for dinner, nor did he spend the night. After a while, Radhika obliged him with some kinky stuff, doing things his wife wouldn't, not that he ever had the courage to ask her.

Two years later, one evening, she told him.

'Someone has asked me to marry him,' she said softly while the two were watching the evening news on television. He switched it off, taken by surprise. He had no idea Radhika was also seeing someone else.

'Do I know him?'

'No,' she replied.

That was a lie.

She had met Philippe on his visit to Delhi while she was employed by K&M. He was a buyer for Galleries Lafayette, and she had picked him up at the airport and later dropped him off a couple of times. On his second visit, he had asked her for her address, and they had been corresponding since. He would phone once in a while from Paris to chat. He had also come to Delhi the previous year after Christmas, and the two had spent a week in Goa on vacation. It was then that he had proposed to her.

Philippe was much older than her, recently divorced with two grown-up children. Radhika did not want to make a hasty decision, though she had always liked him. He was good-looking, stable, and she didn't mind the age difference. But Paris was an entirely different world. The fact that she didn't know a word of French was only one of the problems.

'I hear the French eat snails and frogs,' she said, half-jesting.

Philippe laughed.

'Not all the time,' he replied. 'I love Indian food.'

'I want to think this over,' she told him.

'Why don't you come to Paris before you decide?' he suggested. 'I will pay for the ticket, and you can stay with me.'

She accepted the offer and stayed for a few weeks, telling Kantibhai she was going to Orissa for a family wedding. Philippe showed her the usual sights, and she liked Paris. If she accepted his proposal, she envisioned the possibility of setting up a boutique and starting a business importing ethnic wear from India. The Left Bank, where the young gathered, would be an ideal location. She shared the idea with Philippe, who said he would stand as a guarantor for a bank loan. That made up her mind.

She was disappointed that his flat was smaller than she expected and that there were no servants except for a cleaning lady who came once a week. He explained that things were different in France; much of his earnings went toward alimony, which included the children's education and upkeep.

In Paris, he proposed to her again, this time getting down on his knees.

'*Oui*,' she said, the only French word she knew, other than '*merci*'.

Kanti hadn't suspected anything at all. 'Who is the man?' he asked now, still shaken.

'He lives in Paris,' she said.

Kanti assumed he was an Indian living abroad.

'We'll be getting married there,' she volunteered.

'When do you leave?'

'Next week,' she said.

He was upset by the suddenness of it all and the fact that she had not confided in him about such an important development. He told her as much.

'What about this flat?' he asked.

'I will stay here whenever I come to Delhi.'

Kantibhai was angry but kept his cool. He had bought the place and paid for just about everything in it. He had made the mistake of putting the title in her name and was now in no position to make a fuss or issue a threat. Word could get out, and the last thing he needed was for his wife to find out about Radhika.

He got up, left the keys to the flat on the table, and walked out the door and from her life without saying another word.

Radhika sold the gas agency at a good profit.

In some years, Radhika would become a wealthy woman. She would nurse Phillipe through a year of cancer. When he died, she would move to Montreal and make a greater success there, importing and selling Indian textiles and crafts.

Meanwhile, Kantibhai would slowly get over his bitterness, even the anger and loathing that he felt when he learned of her caste. He felt grateful that she had exited his life so cleanly and completely. He had been freed from the deranging pleasure of the body. Such pleasure that one could easily break every rule and risk disaster and ruin. It was for this reason that, when his little son grew up into a man and fell in love with another unsuitable woman, 'untouchable' in a different way, he felt rage and fear in equal measure.

III

2007–2012

13

'Where is Mohan?' Kantibhai asks one evening just before dinner is served.

'He said not to wait,' Kokilaben tells him. 'He will be eating out.'

'He's eating out a lot these days. It's time we got him married.'

'He is still young,' Kokilaben says, but she's worried too. The last couple of months, their son has been spending a lot of time outside home and the office that he can't satisfactorily account for. 'Friends,' is all he says when she asks.

'How old were we when we got married?' Kantibhai asks as the cook and his helper bring the food out and put it on the table. 'We should start looking for a bride, a nice girl from our community.'

He puts some rice on his silver thali, pours some kadhi on it, adds the cooked vegetables and some oil from the methi achaar and gives the whole thing a good mix with his fingers.

'Otherwise, one of these fast Delhi girls will entrap him,' he continues.

'There are hardly any Gujarati bania families in Delhi,' Kokilaben says.

'I'm aware of that. We'll go to Ahmedabad. Maybe a mill-owner's daughter. We are now richer than they are,' he says with a smile of satisfaction. 'Their havelis are falling apart, one of them got investors and converted his into a hotel. A match with our family will be a boon for someone like that.'

'He won't come to Ahmedabad if we tell him why we are going,' the mother says, knowing her son better.

'I'll tell him we are going on business,' Kantibhai says. 'He can't say no to that.'

For a moment he stops digging into the food.

'Can you imagine some Punjabi or Bihari bride in this house? Some girl who has been shameless before she married and who spends money like it is water? He will be ruined. Everything we have built will be ruined.'

Kokilaben is a little surprised by the vehemence in her husband's tone.

'I think you are worrying too much. Mohan is a good boy,' she says.

Kokila's surprise turns to astonishment and hurt as Kantibhai turns on her with anger.

'What do *you* know?' he snaps. 'Sitting in this house all day, what do you know of the world?'

Her eyes sting with tears. Husband and wife finish their meal in silence.

Two middle-aged men are going up the escalator in the sprawling new mall that has opened in South Delhi's Saket. Some stare at the unusual sight of two Muslim men, traditionally dressed, in a mall. The duo have a small shop selling carpets on the second floor. They once owned a shop in Chandni Chowk but decided to go upscale.

Aziz, the older of the two, is looking down, as he goes up the escalator, at the coffee shop in the ground floor lobby. His eyes fall on a young couple. He taps his companion on the shoulder to draw his attention.

'Isn't that our Zafarbhai's daughter?'

'Yes, I think so,' the other replies.

'What is she doing sitting with a boy in a mall?' Aziz says disapprovingly. 'And why is she without her hijab?'

Kantibhai, Kokilaben and Mohan are having dinner at home.

'Nice to have you join us for dinner for a change,' Kantibhai says to his son, not without sarcasm.

'Sorry, friends' birthdays, promotions, couldn't say no,' Mohan says casually.

Kantibhai digs into the khichdi and stuffed eggplant.

'We are going to Ahmedabad this coming weekend.'

'Okay. Good,' Mohan says.

'A new mall has come up and someone is keen on stocking our line of clothing in his shop,' the father continues. 'We'll check out the place. We can't depend only on exports, we need to expand our Indian market.'

'Good idea,' the son agrees.

'You are coming with us, your mother and me,' Kantibhai adds.

Mohan is surprised.

'Is Baa coming with us?'

'Yes.'

'But we are going on business, right?'

Now the mother intervenes.

'I have not been to see my sister for some time. I've

decided to come along. It's a business trip combined with pleasure.'

Mohan turns to his father. 'Why do you need me?' he says suspiciously. 'I know very little about the Indian market. One of the managers is handling it.'

'No, it is better you came. I'm uncomfortable with these young fellows who have shops in malls.'

Left with no choice, Mohan agrees.

Kantibhai is less keen on going to Ahmedabad than his wife. Kokilaben's younger sister, Shanti, is married into a very wealthy family. He resents his brother-in-law, Ramesh, but is careful to hide it. Though there is little difference financially between the two families, Ramesh and Shanti move in circles in Ahmedabad and elsewhere that he can only envy. Kantibhai knows ministers and senior civil servants in the capital, but he can hardly call them his friends, especially the senior bureaucrats. He lacks Ramesh's sophistication.

Ramesh and Shanti's single-storey bungalow must have cost a fraction of Kantibhai's farmhouse in Chattarpur, more wood and bricks than marble, but it is more admired by their circle of friends. It has been featured in several design and architecture magazines. Kantibhai's tastes are considered too ostentatious, nouveau riche. This doesn't bother Kantibhai as much as the fact that the brother-in-law is a graduate of the prestigious Indian Institute of Management, while he himself had been denied a proper education.

Ellis Bridge, the part of Ahmedabad where Ramesh and Shanti live, lies along the Sabarmati river. The area was developed as Ahmedabad prospered thanks to its cotton mills. The magnificent havelis in the old part of the city were abandoned in favour of modern buildings. Ellis Bridge became an amalgam of posh residential settlements, expensive hospitals and upscale educational institutions.

Ramesh has made his fortune in the jewel business, with showrooms not only in the Indian metros but in a few cities in Europe and the Middle East as well. During Eid he makes a killing in his shops on Bond Street in London and the Dubai Marina. His father was once employed in the business of cutting and polishing diamonds in Surat. When he became skilled, he started a business of his own with an office in Antwerp, the renaissance city in Belgium that is the centre of the world's diamond trade. He prospered and sent his son to the best business school in the country. When the father died Ramesh, the only male child, sold off the diamond business and concentrated on designing and retailing jewellery.

On the evening of Kantibhai and Kokilaben's arrival, there is a small dinner party to welcome them. Ramesh and wife have invited another couple and their daughter, close friends of the family. To Kantibhai's surprise, drinks are offered, premium Scotch. Kantibhai declines, as does Mohan.

'Have a drink, Mohan. I'm sure your father wouldn't mind,' the host presses.

Mohan again declines.

'He is a teetotaler,' Kantibhai intervenes.

Ramesh gives Mohan a knowing smile and pours one for the other guest as well as one for himself. The women are not offered alcohol. A bearer brings them freshly squeezed mosambi juice. All the talking is done by the elders and men and women sit separately.

The two youngsters barely say anything. Shanti says to them, 'You will be bored with us older folk. You don't need to be tied to us.'

The daughter of the visiting couple gets up from the

corner with the cluster of sofas where the women are seated. She goes up to Mohan and introduces herself.

'Hi, I'm Amrita. I think we should leave our elders to their serious talk. Shall we go over there,' she says, indicating a seating area at the other end of the large hall.

Mohan rises and accompanies her.

'Sorry, I should have introduced myself,' he says when they settle into the lounge chairs.

'Don't worry. Gujaratis don't believe in introductions, though they don't mind asking personal questions to people whom they hardly know. It pisses me off when total strangers ask me where I live, where I work, how much I earn.'

She speaks in English and Mohan is taken aback by her use of colourful language. Fortunately, the others are out of earshot. Her English is without the sing-song accent associated with Gujaratis, Amdavadis in particular. She is dressed in jeans, which Mohan finds a bit unusual for a formal dinner, but he is secretly impressed. Amrita has a slender frame and the jeans accentuate her curves. She has let her long hair hang down to her waist.

'You studied abroad, didn't you?'

Amrita ignores the question. She grabs his hand. Mohan senses all eyes are on them.

'Come, I will show you a bit of Ahmedabad,' she says.

It is now past nine and Mohan is unsure how he should respond. He looks towards the others, a bit embarrassed, particularly towards Amrita's parents. It seems fine with everyone, including his own parents. The two walk out the door and towards a red Porsche that stands out among the cars parked outside.

'I've come in my own car,' she says as she opens the door to the passenger seat, 'get in.'

'Wow!'

'My family is loaded,' she says as she starts the engine, 'I'm sure you knew that.'

'No, I didn't. But I'm sure my dad did.'

'Would you like to drive?' she asks.

'No,' Mohan says firmly, 'I have not driven anything like this baby before. I will get us both killed.'

'What brings you to Ahmedabad?' she asks, as she backs out the car.

'Business,' he replies.

'Ha!' she says, 'My dad warned me of the set-up.'

As she drives off, she pushes a button and the top rolls back.

The breeze lifts her hair. She looks beautiful, Mohan thinks. Like a movie star.

'I'm sure you've seen your fill of this godawful city on your previous visits. Let's take a walk by the lake.'

The moon is up, not full but close to it. At the lake, the breeze turns a bit windy. She takes him past the food stalls, still crowded, past the zoo, now closed, past the water rides towards a more secluded spot where they can have some privacy.

'My parents used to bring me here on Sundays in a stroller. My treat was crushed ice on a stick with my choice of syrup poured over it. Supremely unhygienic considering where the ice probably came from. But I never got sick. The place had an elegance and charm that has all but gone,' she says wistfully.

They walk in silence for a while, comfortable in each other's company.

'Do you want to kiss me?' she says abruptly. 'I know where we can go.'

Mohan is shocked. He blushes.

'Look at you!' she says and bursts out laughing. 'I'm joking. I read somewhere that the majority of Gujaratis have never kissed their spouses. It is considered jootha.'

'It's probably true,' Mohan says, delighted by her lack of reserve. 'Many husbands and wives won't drink from the same glass unless it is washed first.'

They find an empty bench facing the lake with trash lying around it.

'I won't marry you,' she says as they sit.

Now it is Mohan's turn to laugh. Spunky girl!

'Who asked you to?'

'I know that is why my parents and I were invited this evening by your maasi. I'm not a fool. My parents kept me in the dark until we left home, they probably didn't want me to get hurt if you rejected me.'

'That's not fair,' Mohan says. 'You beat me to it. I was going to say the same thing to you, maybe not so bluntly. I have no intention of marrying you either.'

Amrita pretends to be offended.

'How rude,' she says. 'Don't you find me attractive?'

'You are beautiful. It's just that there's someone else.'

'Your parents don't approve of her? That's why they brought you here?'

'They don't know,' he says. 'I haven't told them yet. She's not Gujarati. I don't know about my mother, but my father's heart is set on a Gujarati bahu.'

As they walk, Amrita grabs his arm.

'I'm going back to the US,' she says.

'I thought I detected a slight American accent. Are you studying there?'

'No, I've finished. I was at Princeton.'

'I was at Harvard.'

'I wouldn't have guessed,' she says. 'I'm impressed.'

'Don't be. It was just for a summer. Two months, really. A short business administration course. It cost a fortune. I was relieved there were no exams at the end of the course.'

'I like that about you,' she said, 'you are upfront.'

'Truth be told, I am a BA pass from Kirorimal College,' Mohan says.

She is amused.

'Really, a college named Kirorimal?'

'Don't laugh. Amitabh Bachchan studied there,' he tells her. 'Why are you going back to America?'

'I have a boyfriend. We're planning to get married.'

'A gora?'

'Yup! They make the best husbands. They aren't mummy's boys.'

'Do your parents mind?'

'If he'd been Black, they probably would have. The fact that he's White doesn't bother them. It's that I won't be here, with them. You see, I'm the only child, heir to a fortune. They want me in India. And there's no way Paul can fit in here. He's a professor.'

'I hope it works out for you.'

'My leaving is breaking their hearts. But I want to make a life of my own, away from this suffocating place.'

'You don't mind cooking, doing laundry, washing dishes?'

'Of course not. It's very liberating and good therapy. Besides, unlike you guys, white husbands help out around the house. I'll have to get used to that bloody toilet paper, though. I've lived there four years now but I haven't gotten used to that.'

'I used a Campbell soup can. But you can take one of

those spray gun things from here and install it next to the toilet seat,' Mohan suggests.

'I've thought of that. But they can be a pain sometimes. Literally! I think I'll get Paul to add a bidet in the bathroom,' Amrita says.

They continue walking, now with Mohan's arm around her waist. She leans over and kisses him on the cheek.

'You're nice. I like you. You will make somebody happy,' she says.

She tells him that her family had owned mills and spun calico until her grandfather sold out and diversified into pharmaceuticals since there were constant hassles with the worker's unions. 'The mills were losing money and we couldn't meet their demands, however reasonable they were,' Amrita says.

'Tell me about it,' Mohan says.

Amrita misunderstands him and continues. 'Our mills could not compete with small units run from godowns. We tore our place down and, in partnership with a developer, a residential complex was built on the acres where the mills once stood. A swanky pharmaceutical factory was constructed outside the city limits where land was cheaper.'

'Your family is old money?' he asks.

'Of course,' Amrita says. 'My father is a Cambridge graduate.'

'Invite me to the wedding.'

'Seriously? Will you come to New York?'

'I promise.'

'But no. I'm dreaming. I'm sure the wedding will be here. My parents wouldn't have it otherwise. Besides, all our friends there have seen that movie, *Monsoon Wedding*, and they are looking for a big, fat celebration in India.'

'What will happen to this lovely car after you leave?' Mohan asks.

'Do you want it?'

'Of course not,' Mohan says surprised.

'I like teasing you. Bapuji will mothball it for me till after the wedding. He loves my gora but is still hoping I will change my mind and find someone here.'

Mohan is pleased she did not use the word 'Dad'.

It's time to leave. After the two sisters bid each other a tearful 'aavjo', a Mercedes takes the visitors to the airport.

'How can that girl come to meet a prospective groom and his parents in jeans?' Kantibhai says. 'It is simply not done! I'm sorry, Mohan, she's not our type.'

Mohan smiles.

'She seemed nice,' Kokilaben says quietly.

Kantibhai snorts in disagreement.

14

Madhu and Seema are warmly dressed. Winter is approaching. They are sipping cups of piping hot chai at a shop in Chandni Chowk, with sooji halwa straight off the tawa. The corner shop is open on two sides. The street noise is not intrusive, in fact it is rather pleasant.

'I'll hand in my resignation at the end of the month,' Seema says.

Madhu takes this in, she's known this was coming.

'This can't go on,' Seema adds.

'Are you in love with him?' Madhu asks gently.

'I don't know. I like him a lot,' her friend tells her. 'He's very nice, not at all what I had first thought.'

'Does he know how you feel about him?'

'I don't know,' she says frankly.

'What if your Ammi finds out?'

Seema shudders at the thought.

'She won't. I can't do this to her. I have to leave the job and see if I can find something else.'

'Why leave? Just break up with him. Maybe Kantibhai will let you stay, even if the gossip reaches him.'

'You can't be serious?'

'In the front office, they say you are good at your work. Everyone likes you. You have empathy with the workers.

And the workers love you.'

'Don't,' Seema stops her, 'you'll make me cry.'

The two get up. It has started getting dark, time to head home. As they leave, they take in the sweet smell of the halwa being stirred on the large tawa.

'This is not healthy,' Madhu complains.

'But it's delicious.'

On the street they take in the pleasant autumn breeze, a relief after a rather nasty summer.

'I'll hand in my resignation and then tell Mohan,' Seema says, 'I don't want to put him in a difficult situation.'

Seema is about to break into tears. Her friend quickly changes the subject.

'Are you going to the office picnic on Sunday?'

'No.'

'Yes, you are. You are coming with me.'

'It's at their farmhouse in Chattarpur.'

'That's why you're coming. You have to see that house!' Now Madhu teases Seema. 'Maybe it will be the first and last time you see the place you'll be missing out on.'

'Not funny.'

'Has Mohan seen where you live?' Madhu asks.

'No. He always wants to drop me home, but I've told him I live in a very conservative neighbourhood and it will raise eyebrows.'

Madhu holds her friend by the hand. 'That's true.'

———

It is a bright clear day on the spacious lawns of Kantibhai's farmhouse. It is the annual office picnic and the place is crowded with employees from the office and factory with their spouses and children. It is a democratic crowd, from the top executives to humble peons. But everyone knows their place, they congregate among their own in various areas of the lawn.

Only the children are ignorant of the hierarchy. They splash together in the shallow end of the swimming pool under the watchful eye of a lifeguard. Balloons everywhere. Bollywood music blasting. There is a dance floor but no one is on it. Not yet. Camel rides have been arranged for the children and there is also a small Ferris Wheel.

Madhu and Seema are at the food stalls where they're being served street food: chaat, dosas, aloo tikkis, dahi vadas, all from a renowned caterer from Chawri Bazar. After loading their plates, they join their friends seated on garden chairs. The children in the pool nearby are making a racket but they don't mind. It is that kind of a party.

In one corner of the lawns there is a foursome on the tennis court. When the game is over Mohan comes carrying two tennis rackets. He is dressed for the game, somewhat too smartly.

'Anyone for tennis?' he asks brightly, swinging his racket.

There are no takers. He turns to Madhu. 'Come on, we'll play one set.'

'Sir, I don't play. But Seema here does.'

Seema is alarmed. She gives her friend a dirty look.

'Great,' say Mohan, 'let's go.'

'I'm not very good at it,' Seema protests.

Madhu now has a wicked smile. 'It's okay,' Mohan says, 'I'll play at your level.'

This upsets Seema but she says nothing. She points to her sandals. 'I'm not wearing the right shoes.'

'Not a problem,' Mohan says. He signals to one of the

house servants. 'Can you bring some pairs of ladies' tennis shoes from the gym? They're in the locker.'

He says it in a tone that surprises both women. It is unexpected, it is not an order, more a request. Once again, they are pleased to note that he is not the usual, rich brat.

'I'm sure we have a pair your size.'

Soon the two are on the tennis court facing each other.

'I have to see this,' Madhu says to no one in particular, and gets up and moves to the bench inside the tennis court enclosure. Seema is annoyed at being put in this position. The ball boys are house gardeners trained for such occasions. Mohan and Seema do some practice serves. She gives nothing away. When they start, she asks Mohan to serve first.

'Are you sure?' his voice is bordering on condescension.

'Yes,' she replies, 'one set only. Are you okay with that?'

'Fine with me,' he says.

Mohan serves the first ball gently, which Seema returns with ease. The next ball he serves is stronger. Again, Seema returns it smoothly. Mohan is surprised. He takes a patronizing tone.

'I am impressed. I did not know Old Delhi girls could play tennis.'

'I'll show him,' she mutters under her breath but loud enough for Madhu to hear. Her friend grins.

They start playing again. Seema beats Mohan easily in the first game. In the next game, Mohan barely manages to win. Now a small crowd has gathered to watch them play. Some of the female employees cheer Seema on. Some of the male employees are uncertain, the idea of a woman beating their boss on his grounds makes them uncomfortable.

By now Kantibhai and Kokilaben have also been drawn to the game by the commotion.

'*Aa kem ramai*?' Kokilaben asks.

Kantibhai explains the basic rules to her. 'You have to hit the ball over the net and it must fall within the area marked in white.'

He doesn't explain the serve or other finer points of the game. She is satisfied, she has got the basics, enough to follow the game. From time to time her husband adds more information.

Seema wins 6-3 and a few people clap. If Mohan is embarrassed, he does not show it, he takes the loss in good humour.

They go back to the party as he wipes off the sweat.

'I forgot to tell you, she was the college champion,' Madhu says.

'Thanks a lot!'

The parents come and join them. The two women get up.

'Well done, Seema! It was time he was put in his place. He always beats me,' Kantibhai says.

'Thank you, sir.'

Kantibhai turns to Kokilaben. 'This is Seema,' he says, 'she's joined the company recently.'

'Well done, beta,' she says warmly to Seema.

'Aunty, please join us,' Seema says. Someone pulls up a chair for Kokilaben. As she sits, she pauses, takes a good look at Seema.

Kantibhai has already gone off to take care of the guests.

'What a lovely girl,' she says, making Seema blush. 'We will be having dandiya raas here during Navratri, the two of you must come.'

Kokilaben turns to Mohan, 'See that they are sent invitations.'

Mohan is delighted at this turn of events.

'Whatever you say, Baa,' Mohan replies quickly, sealing the deal before his father returns. Kantibhai likes to limit socializing with the staff, he might not have approved.

Madhu and Seema are exhausted by early evening and decide to leave as the lights are switched on. They return home by bus. Madhu is dozing off with her head on her friend's shoulder.

'Dandiya raas? You better go alone,' Seema says nudging her.

Madhu wakes up from the snooze with a yawn.

'Don't be silly. You will come with me. It will be fun,' she says.

Then Madhu realizes what's bothering Seema. 'It's just dancing and partying, there's nothing religious about it. I know a place where we can buy ghagras and other Gujju stuff. It's the dance in which men and women go around in circles with a pair of sticks. No touching.'

'This can't go on. I have to tell him.'

'Are you in love with him?' Madhu asks again.

This time Seema is unable to control her tears.

'I can't do this to Ammi,' she says, 'she has always trusted me. I can't let her down. I must find another job.'

Then she wipes her tears and says firmly. 'We'll go away. Life in the village can't be all that bad. I will hand in my resignation at the end of the month. Then I'll tell Mohan.'

Madhu does not say anything. She knows it is for the best. She gives Seema a hug.

'They grow great mangos in my mother's village,' Seema tells her. 'So you see, it can't be so bad.'

Madhu detects a hint of bitterness. She changes the subject.

'The tennis game was fun, wasn't it? He looked so surprised! Everyone did.'

'I wish you hadn't mentioned my winning the tennis championship in college,' Seema says. 'It was no big deal. It was mostly boys and they are usually lazy. Only half a dozen of us girls played tennis and we were all serious about it. My Abba encouraged me to learn to play, he bought me the racquet. For him it was a small fortune. I guess he wanted me to enjoy the things he missed out on as a child.'

Zafar had grown up in poverty even though his ancestors had been courtiers to emperors. Most of his extended family had packed their bags and taken the train to Pakistan after Partition. Three of his relatives got slaughtered on the way to Lahore, including his father's older brother.

His father was also tempted to cross over with the family but with no savings, he did not have the luxury to venture into the unknown. At least in Delhi they had a roof over their heads. If Zafar's father regretted that decision, he did not let on. He continued working in the kitchen of a hole-in-the-wall restaurant on the road close to the big mosque. When the restaurant closed late at night, he was allowed to take some of the leftovers for the family.

Zafar was sent to an Urdu medium school but plucked out at the age of fourteen to apprentice in a vehicle repair shop. He slept on the floor in their one-bedroom flat and was married at the age of twenty-three to Seema's mother. Both his parents died soon after Seema was born.

Two weeks after the picnic, around noon, Mohan comes down to the floor of the factory where finished garments are stored before being shipped. He is inspecting the inventory and has a clipboard in his hand to take down notes. He hears the sound of someone murmuring from behind one of the racks. It surprises him.

Bismillaah ar-Rahman ar-Raheem

Al hamdu lillaahi rabbil 'alameen

(In the Name of God, The Infinitely Good, The All-Merciful…)

A Muslim prayer? He looks behind the rack. At first, he doesn't recognize the woman wearing a hijab. He takes a closer look. It is Seema. Her eyes are closed as she prays. She turns her head to the right and then to the left.

Mohan quietly withdraws.

On the first night of Navratri, the lawns of Kantibhai's farmhouse are lit up with thousands of traditional diyas made of clay and fuelled with pure ghee. The diyas are large and will stay lit well past midnight, spreading a soft and warm aroma. Servants rush to replace any that flicker in the breeze. The tent house manager had suggested the more fashionable strings of electric lights but he was overruled. They are not Kantibhai's style, he is a traditionalist.

From time to time the sky is lit up with state-of-the-art fireworks. A fusion band has come from Mumbai and is playing Gujarati dandiya music and Bollywood staples. A handful of professional dancers, part of the band, encourage the crowd to get on the dance floor and teach the uninitiated the basic steps and move in endless circles. Some might find this monotonous and repetitive, but everyone is having a good time.

Madhu, more experienced, shows Seema the steps of the dance. She is a good learner and picks it up quickly. They click their dandiyas against those of the men circling around with them to the beat of the music, as if it is the most natural thing to do. There is some flirting on the floor but it is quite harmless and in the spirit of the evening. Security personnel spread themselves out to every corner of the compound to discourage couples from heading towards the bushes.

Around ten, fairly exhausted, Madhu and Seema head for the bar. No one is expecting alcohol and none is served. There are non-alcoholic versions of cosmopolitans and mojitos. Some men have brought hip flasks, mostly vodka. They spike their fruit juices or soft drinks but it is done quietly and with the connivance of the waiters.

Both girls leave it to one of the men behind the drinks stand to mix them something exotic. He crushes some mint leaves in two glasses and minutes later hands them two virgin mojitos.

Inside the house the husband and wife are squatting on the floor and take turns pouring ghee on the sandalwood fire in the metal urn. The priest next to them reads from the Bhagavad Gita. As soon as the puja is over, everyone stands. Kokilaben signals to the office manager and whispers something in his ear. Kantibhai, Kokilaben and Mohan perform aarti in front of the family's idols. The priest's assistant hits the gong. The aarti plate is passed around to the grownups present. Everyone joins in the chant. The priest, in an immaculate silk dhoti, rings the small temple bell.

Om Jai Jagadish hare
Swami Jai Jagadish Hare
(Victory to you, the Lord of the Universe…)

There is a faint sound of the music trickling in from

outside. The office manager looks around and finds Seema on the dance floor, blissfully happy.

'Madam is calling you inside,' the manager tells Seema.

The music is loud. She cannot hear what he is saying.

'Kantibhai's wife wants you to come inside,' he says, this time more loudly.

Seema is surprised. She turns to Madhu who has overheard. The friend shrugs her shoulders, she has no idea what it is all about. Seema hands her sticks to Madhu.

'I will be right back,' she tells her friend and follows the man into the house.

The aarti is in its final stages. The manager whispers in Kokilaben's ear. She turns around and sees Seema standing at the door. She gives Seema a warm smile and motions for her to join them. Mohan too turns around and sees Seema.

Now Seema realizes why she has been summoned. The moment of truth. She turns and flees from the house, much to the consternation of Kantibhai and Kokilaben. Only Mohan knows why.

Seema runs, lifting her ghagra as she does. Tears are streaking down her face as she exits the gate.

Mohan comes out of the house looking for her. Madhu is still on the dance floor with her friends, not realizing that Seema has left without her. Mohan approaches her.

'Where's Seema?' she asks.

Mohan has a good idea. Now it is he who looks like he might break down. 'She left.'

It dawns on Madhu that he now knows.

'She was going to tell you,' she says to him softly. She is not sure he believes her.

Seema is on the road. It is late and dark. She panics but there is no way she is going back in again to look for her friend. She is sobbing. Fortunately, there is no one around. She realizes that Mohan and Madhu will come looking for her. To avoid meeting them she heads towards the nearest bus stand, now more composed.

It is late and the buses have stopped plying. This can be dangerous for her on a deserted road. She is still in her ghagra and men might make assumptions. Should she go back and take one of the buses that the company has organized for the staff? Before she can decide she sees an autorickshaw coming her way. She stops it.

'I already have a passenger, beti,' the driver says kindly, seeing Seema's distress.

'Where do you want to go?' the middle-aged lady in the passenger seat asks.

'Daryaganj, Aunty.'

'I live near here, a few minutes away,' she tells Seema, 'get in. He will drop you after I get off. These deserted streets at night are not safe for women alone.'

Seema hesitates but gets in next to the woman. She is not sure it is a good idea.

'Bhaiya,' the woman says to the driver, 'Drop me home. We are almost there, then you can take beti home.'

When they reach the lady's house near the Chhatarpur temple, she takes down the driver's name from his licence, as well as the number of the rickshaw.

'What's your mobile phone number?' she asks him.

'I don't have one, behenji, I'm a poor man,' the driver says.

'Beti, you will be all right,' the lady says kindly to Seema, 'but, if you wish, you can stay the night here with my family and leave in the morning.'

'Thank you, Aunty, that's very kind of you,' Seema says, 'but I should get home, otherwise my mother will worry.'

On the way there are calls on her phone from Madhu and Mohan. She doesn't pick up. She sends Madhu an SMS: 'Am ok. Going home.' Then she sends another: 'Tell him. Am ok.'

When Seema reaches Daryaganj the driver insists on dropping her at her doorstep where he refuses to take the fare. When he starts the engine Seema presses a five-hundred rupee in his hand.

'This is too much beti, I can't accept this,' he says.

'Diwali is coming up, baba,' Seema says, 'please don't refuse a daughter's gratitude.'

At home she closes the door behind her gently so as not to wake her mother. It is almost midnight, but Jabeen is awake, anxiously awaiting her daughter's return.

'Beta, you are back?' It's her mother's voice from the bedroom.

'Yes, Ammi.'

She had intended to change from the ghagra and choli at Madhu's place before heading home after the party. Now she quickly changes into her sleepwear. She goes to her mother's bedroom quietly, raises the thin blanket and slides in next to her.

'How was the party?' her mother asks.

'Nice, Ammi.'

'Is something wrong?' Jabeen asks instinctively.

'I just want to be with you,' Seema says and hugs her mother.

15

On the first day at work after the Navratri and Dussehra break, Seema is on the factory floor talking to some workers. She looks up and sees that Mohan is in his office above. She picks up the phone to call him but then changes her mind. She excuses herself and goes up to his office and knocks on his door. When she enters, Mohan looks up from his papers.

'Hi. Come in. Sit.'

Seema prefers to stand. Quicker that way.

'Would you like some coffee?' he asks in a neutral tone.

'No thanks, I have to go. Can we meet after work? We need to talk.'

'Okay, how about coffee at six? Same place?'

'Yes. See you then.'

As Seema turns the knob of the door she turns around and looks at Mohan one more time.

Later that day Seema and Madhu are heading to the cafeteria at lunchtime.

'I will say goodbye to him this evening. Tomorrow I will hand in my resignation.'

Madhu is upset when she hears this but does not say anything. It seems like the only course of action.

Mohan and Seema are at a table in the food court on the ground floor of a mall where they usually come to watch movies.

'Sorry,' Seema says after her first sip of the cappuccino.

'Why didn't you tell me when we first met?'

'It took me a long time to find a job and I was afraid to lose it,' she says. 'It was a serious mistake on my part.'

She takes another sip of her coffee; it begins to sink in that she may not see him again.

'And then it was too late. I fell in love.'

Mohan is at a loss as to what to say.

'Does it bother you, the fact that I'm a Muslim?' she asks.

'Of course it does. I would be lying if I said it didn't. You know it makes things complicated,' Mohan says. 'Don't tell me you have no problem with this.'

He hasn't touched his espresso. The waiter comes and asks if they would like to order anything else. Mohan waves him away.

'You don't know my father,' he says.

'At my interview or even later I never lied about my religion, I just didn't give any information that wasn't asked for,' Seema says. She knows this doesn't let her off the hook, so she says honestly, 'I needed employment desperately.'

She gets up. She wants to be home by dinner time. Mohan too gets up and drops a large note on the table and they walk towards the exit. He phones for his car.

'I will hand in my resignation tomorrow,' Seema says, 'I'm sorry for the mess I have got us into.'

Mohan is taken aback by this development.

'Why do you have to do that? No one has to know you're Muslim.'

'But I *am* a Muslim,' Seema says, 'and I'm proud of it,

I had no intention of hiding it forever.'

'Have you no idea how much—' Mohan chokes with emotion and looks away.

Neither of them speaks for moments.

Then Mohan breaks the silence. 'I want to marry you.'

It is now Seema's turn to be surprised.

'Are you mad? You'll marry a Muslim? What about your father?'

'You can convert. I'll talk to him, I'm the only child, he will agree, however reluctantly.'

'Instead, why don't *you* become a Muslim?' Seema is now seething. 'Then my folks won't have a problem either.'

'I can't. I'm a devotee.'

'So am I!' she says more sharply than she intended.

'Seema, be reasonable. You're a woman, it will be easier for you.'

The car is waiting when they get out of the mall.

'Goodbye,' she says.

'I will drop you home,' he offers.

'That won't be necessary,' Seema says and walks away.

That night Seema tosses around in bed. Sleep evades her. Music floats in through the closed window from the public park below, making sleep all the more difficult. She finally gets up and quietly goes to the terrace above. A distraction might help. It is the beginning of winter and there's a lovely nip in the air.

Through a force of habit, Jabeen, on the way back from the bathroom, takes a peek into Seema's room to see if all is well and she is properly tucked in. The bed is empty. She makes her way up to the terrace with one hand against the wall for balance. She knows her daughter will be there.

The music from the concert in the park is loud and clear. Someone is oblivious to the time of the night or just doesn't care. Seema is leaning outwards on the balustrade. Jabeen walks up to her daughter and sees her in tears.

'What is it, beta?'

Seema wipes away her tears. 'Nothing, Ammi.'

'I am your mother,' Jabeen says softly, 'you can tell me. You must.'

Seema decides that this is as good a time as any. Sooner the better. She tells her mother about her desperate search for a job, her fear of moving to the village, Kantibhai's bigotry, the deception she practiced in getting the job, the discarding of the hijab once she was out of the house. And she tells her about Mohan, about falling in love.

Jabeen does not interrupt, lets her finish what she has to say. Then she slaps her daughter across the face. Neither Zafar nor she had ever raised their hands on the children. She feels devastated by that as much by what she has heard.

Jabeen goes down without saying a word.

A few days after the party Mohan is alone at home with his mother.

'Why did Seema leave so suddenly and in the middle of the aarti?' she asks. 'It has upset me quite a bit.'

Mohan too decides to come clean. He tells her that Seema is a Muslim, that she hid the fact in order to get employment at their factory. Until recently he too was unaware that she is not a Hindu.

'What a terrible thing to do,' his mother says, 'your father will be very upset when he finds out.'

Then she looks straight at him, waiting.

'We are in love, Baa,' he tells her, averting his eyes.

'I guessed as much,' she says. Then she adds, 'She is a lovely girl. But you must get rid of her.'

Mohan leaves it to his mother to tell Kantibhai later that evening when he is out. Kokilaben shuts the door of their bedroom before she tells the father. He rages, screams in anger and throws a vase against the bedroom mirror for good measure.

'A Mussalman? I might have accepted a Christian, a white woman, even a *habshi.* But a Mussalman?!'

He sits on the bed, his head in his hands. 'It is my fault. This is my punishment,' he says to himself, softly.

But Kokila hears him.

'Whatever it was, I don't want to know,' she says. Then she leaves the room.

16

A few days later, Javed, Jabeen's brother, turns up in Delhi unannounced. Jabeen has a fairly good idea why he has come and was half expecting him. The word had reached him.

He has arrived by the night train on Sunday morning. After a shower and change he's having breakfast with his sister. Rashid is still asleep. Seema is in her room but is aware of her uncle's presence.

'Where is Seema?' Javed asks, 'Please call her.'

'She is in her room, resting. Let her be. She has been punished. She is a child,' the mother says.

'Did you say a child? She should have been married years ago. What were you thinking? As for that kafir boy, in our village, you know what would have happened to him.'

Jabeen is shocked at this outburst.

'What you saying, Bhai jaan? I know my Seema. She is my flesh and blood. They have not done anything wrong.'

'Tell me about this place where she was working,' the brother asks.

'I will not. It is over, let things be,' Jabeen says.

Javed stops eating and pushes his plate away.

'I was testing you. Now I know I should never have listened to you after Zafar left us,' he says fiercely. 'I have all the information I need. This will end.'

The next day, after vigorous negotiations on the fare, an auto-rickshaw driver agrees to take Javed all the way to the garment factory in Noida. It is a long way off and this part of the capital is unfamiliar to Javed. After further negotiation the driver agrees to wait for him outside the gate, provided he is paid half the return fare in advance.

'I will wait half an hour,' he says, 'after that it will cost extra.'

Javed takes a good look at the façade of the building in front of him. He was not expecting something so grand. These days he is a bit unsteady on his feet and needs the use of his cane to climb the few steps to the entrance. The security guard mistakes him for one of the sub-contractors of the company and lets him in. Javed heads straight towards the receptionist's desk and, with some effort, speaks to her calmly and politely.

'I have come to meet Mohan. Mohan Mehta.'

'Do you have an appointment?' she asks.

'No. I have some urgent business,' Javed responds.

The receptionist looks Javed up and down; she assumes he is one of the tailors to whom the company farms out work from time to time. They all look alike to her with their white kurta, beard and skull cap.

She asks for his name and dials a number.

'I am sorry, Mr Mehta is not in his office right now. He has gone to Delhi on work,' she tells her visitor.

'Is the father in?' Javed asks.

While she is dialling Kantibhai's number he casually asks her where the senior Mehta's office is.

'Second floor,' she tells him.

Javed does not want his presence announced. He will have to explain himself and the business that has brought him here. He spots the elevator and swiftly walks towards it. By the time the receptionist looks up he has already pressed the elevator button. She is alarmed.

'Bhaiya, you can't go up without an appointment,' she shouts, now on her feet.

He is already in the lift and, with a grin, waves his stick at the hapless receptionist.

She presses a button under her desk and shouts at the security standing at the entrance.

'Stop him!'

The guard decides not to wait for the next elevator going up and instead takes the stairs on the run. He is not young, a bit overweight. By the time he reaches the second floor Javed is nowhere to be seen.

'Where has the bloody man gone?' he says to himself as he calls the receptionist on his cell phone.

Having reached the floor, Javed asks a passing employee for Kantibhai's office. He is now holding the cane more menacingly. He locates the office and does not bother with the secretary sitting outside the cabin, he marches past her and bolts the door behind him.

Kantibhai is at his desk and speaking on the phone. First, he does not know what to make of this intrusion. He asks the person on the other end to hold on. Then the threat dawns on him and he puts the phone down.

'Who are you?'

From the man's garb and his angry eyes, he has a fairly good idea that this has something to do with Seema and Mohan.

The visitor is in no mood for formalities. '*Haramzada*, how dare you!' Javed shouts. He swings the cane over his head as he approaches the desk. Kantibhai panics.

'Security,' he shouts and at the same time presses hard several times on the round bell on his desk. It is unnecessary. His secretary is already on the case. The outer office is now overrun with security. One guard with a rifle uses the butt to try to break down the door, without success.

Javed strikes Kantibhai's desk hard with his cane. It is more for effect than anything else. He has no intention of harming the man. Now Kantibhai gets up from his desk and tries to head for the door. Javed blocks him.

'Tell your son to keep away from my niece,' Javed says, still swinging his cane. Kantibhai's eyes are fixed not on the man but on the cane.

He is about to respond that the niece is a gold digger but thinks better of it. This is not a good time. Javed goes around the table and occupies the man's chair. He puts his legs on the desk.

'Keep away from the door,' he says and then looks around. 'You have a nice office.'

'You like it?' Kantibhai asks.

He begins to like the man, a kindred spirit protecting his own.

Javed sees framed portraits of five well-known public figures, Mahatma Gandhi, Vallabhbhai Patel, Morarji Desai and the current prime minister, Manmohan Singh, on the walls. There is also a portrait of Mohammed Ali Jinnah.

Pointing at the last one with his cane, he asks, 'Why him?'

'It's a long story,' Kantibhai says, now calm, realizing that the man will not harm him.

'He too was a Gujarati, like the other four,' Kantibhai tells him. 'But he did the country an enormous service by taking most of the Muslims out of here. For that he deserves to be recognized.'

Javed lets the remark go and without saying anything more gets up, walks to the door of the cabin and opens it to leave.

The security have brought an axe by now and are ready to tear the door down.

'Let him go,' Kantibhai tells the small crowd assembled outside.

'*Haramkhor*,' he says softly.

'What!' Javed asks.

'The word is *haramkhor*, not *haramzada*,' Kantibhai says.

It brings a smile to Javed's face. Even he has to admit: this man is something.

Everyone clears the way. Madhu has not got up from her desk this entire time, but she is aware of what has happened. She goes to the ladies' room and sobs.

The three-wheeler has kept his word. Javed climbs in with some effort.

'Let's go. I am done here.'

That evening Javed is having tea with his sister on the terrace.

'You should start packing. We will leave as soon as I have sorted out the affairs of this place,' he says.

Jabeen has been expecting this.

'I have been making enquiries. You will get good rent for this place,' Javed says, 'or you can sell it.'

'Javed bhai, we have decided we will stay here,' Jabeen says. 'I have spent more than half my life here. I have friends here. The tailors bring me work they can't handle and now women have started coming directly to me. We are comfortable.'

She has surprised herself with the way this has all come out. She has spoken clearly and firmly.

'Besides,' she continues, 'I want Seema to marry here. There are lots of nice, educated boys in Delhi. The village is not the place for her.'

'Muslims?' Javed asks.

Jabeen does not understand the question.

'Are these boys Muslims?'

'Yes, Muslims. Sunni.'

Javed sighs. His little sister can be stubborn.

'It is your decision. I can't force you. I hope you know that we are always there for you.'

Jabeen is touched.

'Bhai jaan, we have always known that.'

Now they see Seema standing behind them at the terrace door. She comes up to Javed and weeps on his shoulder. Javed tenderly takes her in his arms.

'Thank you, Mamu.'

There is a look of worry on Javed's face that Seema does not see. His eyes tear up.

17

Mohan and Seema get out of a taxi. Mohan pays the driver, loads two suitcases on a trolley and they both head towards the airport's departure gates.

'Let me have your passport,' Mohan says.

Seema hands it over and they clear the entrance security and queue up in the 'economy' line. When they board and are seated, Mohan puts a reassuring hand on Seema's shoulder.

'Everything will be all right,' he assures her.

They are casually dressed, the hijab she wore when they boarded is now in her handbag.

When they land in Dubai they are met by Ashok Chawla, Mohan's chum from his Kirorimal College days, and his wife, Priya. Ashok had migrated to the UAE after graduation and has a mid-level position at a British-owned bank. Seema has not met the couple before, but the wife immediately puts her at ease with a warm hug.

'Mohan is family,' she tells her.

'Thank you, Ashok, for offering to put us up. We will move out as soon as I find a job,' Mohan tells his friend.

'Don't be silly,' Ashok says, 'stay as long you want. There is plenty of room.'

When they reach Ashok's flat Mohan, to his discomfort,

finds that the seven-year-old daughter has shifted into her parent's bedroom to make room for their guests.

A week later, Mohan and Seema move into a more modest place of their own, within walking distance from his friend. The wife takes Seema shopping and pays with her credit card.

'You can pay us back once you are settled,' Priya says.

Mohan and Seema are amazed that just about everyone they see on the streets is from the sub-continent, hardly any Arabs in sight. Their hosts greet quite a few of the people in the neighbourhood.

Through his connections Ashok finds Mohan work as a cashier in one of the shops in a mall. Seema, for her part, has no problem landing a sales position in one of the boutiques in the same mall. They take the bus together both ways.

'Tomorrow is our day off. Let us explore the desert,' Mohan tells her after a few weeks. They really haven't had a break since arriving. With Ashok's help they organize a sightseeing tour. The tour bus takes them to the sand dunes around Liwa Oasis near Abu Dhabi. Neither of them has seen anything quite like it.

'Let's go for a camel ride,' Mohan suggests.

Seema is horrified at the idea.

'You go,' she says, 'I will wait for you here, maybe walk around.'

'No, you will come with me,' Mohan says. 'I tell you what, we will go on one together. You hold on to me.'

'Please go alone. I'm scared.'

The tour guide hears them and assures them that it is perfectly safe. The Arab knows Hindi, of sorts. He tells them someone will be accompanying them throughout. Seema is persuaded. When a camel is brought to them Mohan asks the owner the name of the camel.

'Humphrey,' he replies.

Mohan gives him a quizzical look.

'It was his mother's idea,' the man says with a grin.

Mohan realizes his leg is being pulled. He gets on the camel first and helps Seema mount behind him. When the camel gets up Seema screams, partly in delight. The owner of the animal holds the reins from the ground and leads the camel towards the dunes.

All is well until he lets go of the reins and gives it to Mohan to hold while he goes behind the dunes for a pee. For no reason the camel takes off at a gallop. The two hold on for dear life but Seema slips from the saddle. Mohan grabs her hand to steady her but both fall.

That's when Mohan wakes up in a cold sweat. He can't sleep after that and goes for a walk in the lawns of the farmhouse. He tires himself walking, then comes back to his room and sleeps, a dreamless sleep.

Seema's resignation is accepted. She expects a salary deduction for not giving advance notice but there is none. Mr Saxena is sorry to let her go. She was efficient but what drew the management's notice was the way she handled the staff on the factory floor, her concern for them and their family's well-being. Some of the wage-earners at the lower levels, sweepers and cleaners, come from jhuggis in the surrounding area, barely able to make ends meet. They cannot afford to send all their children to school, the older boys find street work to help with the expenses and educate their younger siblings. Those without work often end up with their sons taking drugs or snatching gold chains from the necks of women riding pillion on their husband's two-wheelers.

At the end of the month Seema comes to the office to collect her last pay cheque. No attempt is made to persuade her to stay. The goodbyes at the cashier's office are perfunctory.

Once outside the gate she decides to splurge on an auto-rickshaw ride to take her home. Before she gets in, she turns around and looks at the building where she worked for many months.

'Goodbye, Kantibhai,' she says to herself.

Across the bridge she enjoys the strong breeze that plays havoc with her uncovered hair. To her surprise she is in a great mood. She taps the driver on his shoulder.

'Bhaiya, please hurry,' she says, impatient to get home.

A few weeks after Seema hands in her papers Mr Saxena picks up the phone and calls the branch manager of K&M's bank in Noida. They are one of the branch's biggest customers and they also bring in precious dollars and euros that earn the branch brownie points with the bank's head office in Bombay. A citation to this effect is proudly displayed in the manager's office.

Mr Saxena tells the manager about Seema's resignation without going into the reason. He requests him to find her a position in the bank and that he had to let Seema go despite her excellent performance. It is the first time a request of this nature has come from K&M.

'I will get back to you soon,' the manager assures him.

A week later Mr Saxena gets a call to send Seema to the bank's northern head office in Gurgaon for an interview. She is advised to bring all the pertinent papers and a written recommendation from him. Mr Saxena places a call to Seema.

'Thank you, Uncle,' she says. Now that she is no longer with the company, she has no problem addressing the older man that way. She is deeply touched and aware that he may get into trouble with Kantibhai.

The interview at the bank is short. The head of HR goes through her education records, asks a few questions about her interests and family background. He likes her demeanor—polite, straightforward and dignified. What clinches matters is the strong recommendation from the management of K&M, one of their most valued customers. Seema is told the salary they are offering and her assignment.

'Is that acceptable?' the interviewer asks.

'That is fine, sir,' she replies. The salary is more or less the same as what she had at K&M, but the perks are better.

'When can you start?'

'Whatever suits you, sir,' she says.

'You can start on the first of next month,' he says.

Seema agrees. It will give her a few weeks to get over her stress since breaking with Mohan.

The distance to Gurgaon from home worries her, she will have to change buses twice and take the Metro, too. But she is told that the bank has a shuttle service that picks employees in the morning and drops them to the nearest Metro station at the end of the day.

The interview is over before noon. She picks up a new number for her cell phone from a shop in a mall and heads home.

18

'We will have to do something about Mohan.'

It is evening. Kantibhai has showered and changed into a khadi kurta, as he always does. He is exhausted, both by work at the factory as well as domestic developments. The husband and wife are upstairs in the family room. The television is on at low volume, and they are watching the early evening news on one of the Hindi channels.

'I wonder if that girl in Ahmedabad is still available,' he adds, as he keeps switching channels.

'My sister says she has returned to America,' Kokilaben tells him. 'The family is disappointed that it didn't work out with Mohan.'

'Why was that, you think?' he asks.

'From what I heard, neither Mohan nor the girl were interested in each other. Say what you will, Seema is a lovely girl.'

This does not help Kantibhai's mood.

'She made a fool of us. I don't want to hear about her again. I almost got killed because of her.'

'Don't exaggerate,' Kokilaben says. 'You told me yourself he was more thunder than rain.'

Kantibhai has a plan and has to act swiftly. He gets his exports manager to ring some of their buyers in the US. He asks for suggestions of top colleges in America that have courses in fashion design and textile trade. He has concluded that some time spent abroad by his son will be good for all concerned. Kokilaben is distressed when he tells her of this plan; it will keep their son away for more than a year at least, but she knows better than to argue.

Mr Saxena receives several suggestions in various parts of America but there is one school that keeps coming up in most recommendations. Parsons School of Design located in Greenwich Village, Manhattan. He does some research and is impressed by the college's alumni. It is a powerhouse in its field, benefitting from the fact that New York is America's hub for the garment trade. The college sends information about it together with an application form.

'We are sending you to New York for further studies,' Kantibhai announces at the dinner table once the college has offered admission.

Mohan looks to his mother who is bent over her plate. She says nothing and doesn't look up.

'We are sending you to a fashion school,' Kantibhai adds.

He signals for a servant to bring the large envelope lying on the coffee table. He hands it to Mohan.

'This is the prospectus of the best fashion school in America,' he tells Mohan. 'Read it carefully and fill out the application form.'

Mohan is surprised by this unexpected development, but finds the idea of studying abroad attractive. He's always felt that he had missed out on this experience when his father insisted he join the company after his Bachelor's at Kirorimal.

'When do I go?' he asks.

'Apparently, right away. They have something called a semester system that allows students to join any time, as long as you fulfil the required number of semesters,' Kantibhai says. 'It is all very confusing to me. Mr Saxena will explain it to you. You will have to fill out a visa application too, of course.'

Mohan rings Seema again that evening but he doesn't through. He has called several times since she left K&M but the phone has never rung. He has considered turning up at her flat unannounced but good sense has always prevailed in the end. He has yet to meet her family and has no idea what she has told her mother.

Reluctantly, he asks Madhu to come to his office. This too, he knows, is a bad idea, but he is desperate. When she enters, he tells her to close the door behind her. He cuts to the chase.

'How is Seema?' he asks.

Madhu has always liked Mohan and is aware that she is partly to be blamed for the situation her friend and Mohan are in.

'She's fine, sir,' she says. That 'sir' cannot be avoided in an office situation. She tells him about Seema's new job at the bank, something the company manager neglected to tell him.

'I'm glad to hear that,' he says, genuinely happy for Seema, 'I've tried to get in touch with her, but it I think she has changed her number.'

Madhu is at a loss how to respond. Mohan is tempted to ask if she has Seema's new number but does not. That will put Madhu in a spot.

'Please tell her I'm going to America for further studies, and I would like to talk to her before I go.'

'I will tell her that, sir,' Madhu says.

He doesn't hear from Seema.

Mohan takes a non-stop flight from Delhi to Newark airport. Kantibhai has instructed the office to get a business-class ticket for his son, but Mohan insists on flying economy. He also insists that there should be no farewell party at the office.

A havan at home, restricted to the immediate family, cannot be avoided. He has tears in his eyes when his mother puts a vermilion tika on his forehead. He knows his departure is breaking her heart. Kantibhai steps out into the lawns, not in tears but close. Mohan heads for the airport alone in the family car.

When he lands, he is met by a young man holding a placard with his name. Barbara Elliot, the lead buyer of a major department store with which K&M does business has sent Hamilton Amerasinghe, a Sri Lankan on their staff, to receive him. Hamilton takes him to a three-star hotel in mid-town that has been booked for him until he finds accommodation. Before the Sri Lankan leaves, he hands Mohan a prepaid SIM card for his cell phone, and his phone number.

'I've been asked to take care of you until you settle down,' Hamilton says. 'You can call me any time, twenty-four hours.'

'How do I get to Greenwich Village?' Mohan asks the concierge the next morning.

He mispronounces the name but the man understands. He has heard it pronounced worse.

'Where in the village do you wish to go?' he asks.

The concierge pulls out a tourist map of Manhattan, marks the location of Parsons in yellow and hands it to him. He also marks the location of the hotel on Lexington Avenue.

'You can take the downtown bus from across the street or walk there. For a young man like you it should take less than an hour.'

The folding map is his to keep. He decides to walk. It is a pleasant day. With the streets named numerically he has no trouble finding the college. He is already beginning to like New York.

The clerk at the admission desk is expecting him and hands Mohan a pile of brochures that inform him where his classes will take place, and where the orientation for new students is happening that day. To his disappointment, he is told that the students' residence hall is full. But he is given a list of places in the neighbourhood where rooms might be available.

Lack of accommodation is an unexpected development. He makes a call.

'I'll meet you at the hotel this afternoon,' Hamilton tells him. 'Will five be okay?'

Hamilton Amerasinghe is more or less Mohan's age.

'I wouldn't worry too much. We'll find something,' he says. 'In any case, staying in the dorms is not a great idea. The rooms are cramped and you'll have to share, probably with a white guy.'

'What do you suggest?' Mohan asks.

'Are you a vegetarian?'

'Yes.'

'I guessed as much. I live in Queens, across the river,' Hamilton says. 'I think you should look for a place there. For the price you pay for a dorm room you can have an apartment of your own. Tell you what, I'll come on Saturday morning and we'll go house hunting.'

That weekend they hop on a subway train at 42nd Street and get off at the Roosevelt Avenue station in Jackson Heights.

'You'll love this place,' Hamilton promises.

When they get down from the elevated tracks Mohan is amazed, it's as if he has landed in Delhi's Lajpat Nagar. All the shops seem to be run by Indians, but Hamilton tells him there are, in fact, an equal number of Bangladeshis and Pakistanis in businesses. All cheek by jowl and all getting on with each other splendidly.

Mohan spots a paan shop. The price of one paan is enough to buy a person a whole meal in Delhi. He tells Hamilton that is outrageous.

'You must stop converting the dollar prices into your rupees,' his friend suggests. 'The rich may be richer back home but the poor and the wage earners are better off here.'

There is a supermarket that sells karelas, bhindis and every imaginable vegetable that would have delighted Mohan's mother.

'The produce is not from India. These vegetables are flown in daily, mostly from Kenya, though some enterprising South Asians have started growing them in Florida. The ghee in those cans comes from Netherlands.'

Hamilton is enjoying his role of a tour guide. The two walk from one end to the other of the main drag, past storefronts announcing 22-carat jewellery and shops that sell appliances, shoes, luggage at discounted prices. At lunchtime they order dosas at the Jackson Diner.

Hamilton pulls out a copy of the latest *Desi News*, a weekly paper, that he has picked from a pile outside a grocery store, and opens it to the rental listings page.

'We should look for a place within walking distance from here,' he advises. 'The rents will be affordable. You can eat here or pick up frozen vegetarian dishes from the Patel Supermarket next door. If you put the packets in the deep freeze, they'll stay edible forever.'

The two of them visit several places on the listing until they settle on one that fits Mohan's needs. The flat belongs to a Korean couple, Mr and Mrs Park, who live in the same building. They bought the place for their son who is in college in New Hampshire. It is fully furnished, though in Mohan's eyes, the furnishings are tacky. The plastic roses in a vase and the printed curtains bother him. But the fact that it comes furnished—refrigerator, utensils, television, air-conditioning, a sofa set, a bed, a telephone—is a huge plus point. Mr and Mrs Park, frugal people, don't want to leave the flat vacant for the son until he finishes college, he can stay with them when he comes for his summer break.

The bedroom is small and its windows open on to the red brick wall of the building next door. But the rent is reasonable and the middle-aged couple who speak little English seem nice. Almost all residents in the building are Asians, a healthy mix of noisy, television-hooked Chinese, Koreans and Filipinos with a few Indians and Pakistanis. The smell of curry will not pose a problem. There are a few white residents, they are older and two of them in wheelchairs.

'What do you think?' Hamilton asks Mohan when they are back on the street.

'I like it,' Mohan says. He is in fact relieved that he does not have to share a room with another student in a dormitory. They turn back, take the elevator and ring the Parks' bell again.

On Monday, Mohan opens an account in a bank close to Parsons. He is surprised at how easily it is done. No recommendations are required, just a signature sample, payment for a blank cheque book and a token deposit. He e-mails the bank's direct deposit information to his father and the next day money is transferred, enough to last him several months. He moves into the new apartment on the agreed weekend with his two suitcases.

A few days after he has moved in, the buyer of the department store rings him.

'I believe you've settled down. Please call me if I can be of any assistance,' Barbara says.

Mohan curses himself. He has neglected to get in touch with her since he arrived.

'I'm sorry, Mrs Elliot, I should have called to thank you for sending Hamilton to the airport to meet me,' he says and adds a white lie, 'I've been a bit busy.'

'Not to worry. Hamilton tells me you've found a nice apartment,' she says. 'I'm calling to invite you for lunch at my place next Saturday. Are you free?'

'I am,' he replies.

This is unexpected.

'Good. I'll also invite Hamilton,' Barbara says, 'you can come together. Call me when you leave Grand Central and my husband will meet you at Hartsdale.'

Hamilton is surprised to be included in the invitation from Barbara. He is way out of her league, a back-room clerk at the department store. Then he figures out why he has been invited—to accompany Mohan on a trip he may not be able to negotiate on his own.

At the station Mohan insists on paying for both day-return tickets as a way of thanking his new friend. He buys a bunch of flowers from a kiosk and then rings Barbara to tell her the time of the train's departure.

True to her word, her husband is at the platform to receive them. He recognizes them easily since they are the only Asians getting off at Hartsdale, a posh white ghetto with a sprinkling of successful non-whites, mostly investment bankers and doctors. They cross the bridge over the tracks to reach the car. Mark Elliot is easy going and likable, he asks Mohan how he is settling down.

'Barbara never stops talking about your father. Kanty? Is that how you pronounce his name?' he asks as they drive off. 'She likes doing business with you guys.'

When they reach the home, Barbara and the couples' two boys, both teenagers, are waiting at the door to greet them, excited at having foreign visitors. The house is detached and on two floors. There is a patio with a table and chairs at the back overlooking a swimming pool. It is a lovely day and Barbara suggests that they sit there while she prepares lunch.

'What will you like to drink?' Mark asks, rubbing his hands.

Hamilton and Mohan say they will have Coke.

'Ignore them Mark, open a bottle of Chardonnay,' Barbara shouts from the kitchen, 'I know they both drink.'

A little later she joins them and pours herself a glass.

'I'm sorry I couldn't meet you when you arrived,' she says brightly. 'I hope you guys are starving. I've made fettuccini alfredo.'

She assures Mohan the dish is vegetarian.

'It's pasta with cream, butter and garlic with parmesan cheese. You'll like it.'

She had laid the table indoors but now she changes her mind. They will eat on the patio. Why waste a good day? The children help her lay the table. Mohan is impressed.

Besides the pasta there is salad vinaigrette with lettuce plucked from the family's small garden. The apple pie comes from the local supermarket. It is the best meal Mohan has had since he arrived in New York and he tells Barbara as much. She picks up his plate and gives him a second helping of the pie.

'You don't have be shy in this house,' she says, 'I put on weight every time I return from Delhi and your mother is to be blamed for that.'

Hamilton too makes the most of the first home-cooked meal in a long while. As soon as lunch is over Mark excuses himself, changes and goes off to play tennis at his club.

'He is a real estate agent and works hard five days a week. Tennis helps him unwind,' Barbara says.

She tells the boys to look after the guests while she does the dishes. Hamilton gets up right away.

'I will help you,' he says and follows her into the kitchen.

The boys are curious about India and bombard Mohan with questions.

'Can you do the rope trick?' the older one asks.

'No, but I can do card tricks if you have a pack of cards.'

They certainly do. Mohan is good with the tricks, most of them picked up when he was their age. He makes cards disappear, changes spades into diamonds, tells them the suit of the card lying face down. The sleight of hand makes the boys shout with astonishment.

'How did you do that?'

'Magic,' he says with a smile.

At the end he shows the boys how the tricks are done and encourages them to try doing them. When it is time to go the boys ask their mother if Hamilton and Mohan can come again.

'Of course they can,' she says.

She drops them at the station in her car in time for the next train heading to Manhattan.

Mohan is invited often to Hartsdale after that. It becomes his second home. Now he can go on his own, Hamilton is not invited. At Thanksgiving Barbara makes spinach quiche for him, checking first if he has problems with eggs. He loves the stuffing made separately for him but does not touch the turkey. He watches American football with Mark and the boys who explain the rules of the strange game.

He helps Barbara set the table and by now has learnt to volunteer to help wash the dishes afterwards. On some visits he sleeps overnight on the convertible sofa. Their home becomes a home away from home for him. When he tells his anxious parents about it, they are pleased.

A few months after arriving he calls Amrita, all the while debating whether or not to—he doesn't want to be an intrusion. His presence in New York takes her by surprise and, after consulting her fiancé, Paul, she invites him over for an evening meal.

She is sharing the place in Tribeca with Paul, who is a tenured professor at Columbia. She has found herself a job as the manager of an art gallery in Chelsea.

Amrita has prepared a Gujarati meal herself. Only the roti packet and shrikand she has had delivered from a shop in Little India, a cluster of South Asian restaurants and grocery shops at the unfashionable end of Lexington Avenue. Paul helps her lay the table.

Mohan announces it all delicious, as good as his mother's.

Amrita tells him of a Gujarati restaurant on Manhattan's Third Avenue run by a pair of ladies from New Jersey, in case he gets a craving.

Afterwards Amrita shows him around their apartment. From the living room there is a clear view of the Statue of Liberty and from one of the bedrooms, that of the Empire State Building. Both are lit up.

'We wanted to buy a one-bedroom place but I didn't want Papa and Baa to stay in a hotel when they come visiting,' Amrita says. 'So we bought a two-bedroom. My parents wanted to pay for it, but Paul would not hear of it.'

'That's good of him.'

'These Jews are like Gujjus,' Amrita says, 'all mothers' boys but they make better husbands.'

Amrita tells him that she doesn't encourage other visiting friends and relatives to stay with them.

'Once you start there's no end to it.'

Afterwards Amrita walks with him to the elevator. 'How's it going with the girl you were keen on?' she asks.

'We broke up,' he says.

'Then get over it,' she says.

He is ready to cry. Now she is alarmed.

'What happened?'

'My father objected to our relationship,' he says.

After a moment of silence, he lets it out. 'She's Muslim.'

Now Amrita is concerned. This is unexpected.

'If you are not in a hurry to go home, come back in and we'll talk,' she says kindly.

When they return to the apartment Paul has already retired for the night.

'Will you have coffee?' Amrita asks.

'I would love some tea if you can make it Indian style.'

'I don't have chai masala but I can add ginger and elaichi,' she volunteers.

'Thank you. I miss chai.'

When Amrita is back from the kitchen with the cups, Mohan tells her the story.

'I didn't know she was a Muslim until it was too late. By then I'd fallen in love with her. Seema is lovely in every way.'

'You must have been misled by the name. Didn't she tell you she was Muslim when you met her?'

'No, but there was a good reason. She desperately needed the job in our factory and she'd been warned about my father's intense dislike for Muslims.'

'And you, would you have dated her if you knew?'

'No,' he says. 'My feelings towards them had been influenced by my upbringing. I didn't hate them, but it was clear that their world and ours could never really meet.' He stops, as if surprised by what he has just said. When he speaks again, there is a hint of sadness in his voice. 'I'm ashamed to say it, but my father thought the rioters who killed Muslims after Godhra didn't deserve any punishment. I can't bring myself to believe he supported the killings, but he felt Hindus had been provoked. It was revenge.'

'And your mother?' Amrita asks.

'She can't hate anyone. But she would always refer to them as "those people". I think that became my attitude as well.'

'I'm not surprised,' Amrita says, 'I saw that all around me, in our extended family. Fortunately, my parents were different. My best friend in the convent school I went to was Sadia. We had Muslim families for dinner all the time and when they invited us back, they made vegetarian dishes for us, cooked the way Muslims do. They were of our background, owners of pharmaceutical factories, professors and artists. All that has changed,' she says wistfully.

'We have never had Muslim guests in our home,' Mohan says.

'I remember my father's cousin telling him he was a traitor to his own community, a traitor to all Hindus because he continued to meet his Muslim friends after the train was burned in Godhra,' Amrita says. 'The pogrom carried out across Gujarat was horrible, but people like that uncle were happy with it. I'm not even sure what happened in that train at Godhra. Some say it was Muslim terrorists, some say it was an accident, others that it was a conspiracy hatched by Hindu fanatics. None of that matters, if you ask me, because the guilty were not caught, nor will they ever be, but hundreds of innocent people were butchered, women brutalized and raped. And the police allowed the mobs to loot and kill. I can't believe the police did this without orders from above. I toured the area with my friend soon afterwards. It was a poor part of the town, a ghetto of which I had only been vaguely aware. The stories that we were told still give me nightmares.'

She looks at Mohan. He hasn't touched his tea. 'I'm sorry,' she says, 'I can't forget that time of madness. I get carried away.'

'No. I needed to hear this,' Mohan says. 'I wish someone had told people like us, sitting safe and smug in Delhi, what was being done in our name. I wonder what Seema and her family must have felt then…Sorry, I'm boring you with my problems again. It's just that I don't have any friends I can talk to like this. Thank you for being a friend.'

Amrita puts her hand on his. 'You're a good guy, Mohan. I think you'll do the right thing in the end.'

19

A Mercedes has a hard time passing through the narrow lanes of the old city. Live chickens cluck loudly in protest in their cramped cages while motorcyclists shout impatiently to get past the slow-moving car.

Kokilaben is in the back seat, curiously looking out of the window. The uniformed driver is unhappy to be in the area, worried about denting his precious car.

'Madam, let us go back,' he suggests, 'this is no place for someone like you.'

She will not hear of it. The lady is made of stronger stuff. The driver manages to find a temporary parking space. He gets out and asks for directions from a chai shop owner who points out the way. Everyone seems to know everyone in this neighbourhood. The driver heads towards the back of the grand mosque.

Kokilaben rolls down the window for a better view of Masjid-i-Jehan-Numa, commonly known as Jama Masjid. She has not seen it this close before. For a moment she thinks of getting out to take a closer look, but the thought passes quickly. She knows her employee at the wheel will not allow it.

Once they pass the market and enter the residential area the traffic is much lighter. The car gathers some speed. At the staircase leading to Jabeen's flat the driver gets out and opens the door for Kokilaben.

'I will come up with you,' he says with some determination.

'Anandji, you wait here and look after the car,' she replies, 'I will be fine.'

Kokilaben makes her way up the short flight of stairs and is pleasantly surprised how easily she has managed it.

When Mohan called on her cell phone the previous afternoon, she had answered, her heart racing. It would have been about two in the morning for him. What could have happened? He had said he just wanted to hear her voice, because he missed her. They had spoken, and although he hadn't said it, she could sense that his heart was still broken. And that had broken hers. She had made the decision even as she put down her phone.

And here she is now, climbing up to a door she never imagined she would enter.

Jabeen is cooking in the kitchen. She stirs the pot on the stove before getting back to kneading the flour for rotis when she hears the doorbell ring. Who can that be? Seema, who is in the small living room, puts down the book she is reading and opens the door.

She could have been knocked down with a feather. Her eyes tear up. She instinctively bends low and touches Kokilaben's feet, a gesture not common in her community. Kokilaben puts a hand on the girl's head in blessing. She is a bit out of her breath from the climb.

'Can I come in?'

'Ammi!' Seema shouts.

'Who is it?'

The tone of Seema's voice makes Jabeen leave what she is doing and come to the living room. Before Seema can say anything, Jabeen senses who Kokilaben is.

'Behenji, please sit,' she says.

She is lost for words. And now she is embarrassed at the state of the ancient sofa and the fact that she is in her house clothes.

'Seema has told me so much about you,' she says.

Jabeen pulls a chair and sits next to the visitor while Seema hurries to make tea. Kokilaben looks around.

'You have a nice place,' she says, 'When I was little, we lived in a place like this. It was a chawl, but clean and intimate. It was before my father succeeded in business. I remember those years as a child in a small town as some of my happiest.'

'I'm glad you came,' Jabeen says. 'You people have been so kind to my daughter.'

Seema has returned with two cups and a plate of salted biscuits.

'I have not added sugar,' she tells her guest.

'Not to worry, beti, I will add it myself,' Kokilaben says with a smile. 'All Gujaratis are not diabetic.'

Seema remains standing until Kokilaben tells her to sit next to her.

'How are you, beti? I hear you have a nice job.'

'Yes, Aunty.'

Kokilaben turns to Jabeen.

'You have a lovely daughter. I wish I had one like her.'

Kokilaben now notices that Jabeen's hands are covered with flour. Jabeen is embarrassed. Everything was so unexpected. It had escaped her mind to wash her hands. She should have excused herself and changed.

'I am sorry to have disturbed you, I should have called ahead instead of just turning up like this. I won't stay long.'

'No, Behenji,' Jabeen protests, 'you honour us by your

presence. I don't know what would have happened to us if Seema had not got the job in your company.' She gets up. 'I will be back in a minute,' she says.

She goes to the kitchen and washes her hands in the sink. As she is leaving, she realizes that the pot is still simmering. She turns off the gas. She looks into the pot and quickly shuts it again. There is a faint smell of cooked meat.

'What shall I do with this?' she mutters to herself.

She picks up the pot and places it in a cupboard. She opens the window wide, takes a piece of cloth and tries to drive away the smell.

'What have you been making?' Kokilaben asks when Jabeen returns.

'Rotis,' she replies. 'Please stay for dinner. I will make some sabzi.'

Kokilaben looks at her watch. 'It's almost six. I must be off.'

There is a pause. Jabeen puts her hand on Kokilaben's. 'Please have dinner with us,' she says again.

It is a reckless offer and Seema, standing nearby, is stunned. Their dinner is that pot of meat.

Kokilaben is tempted. She has been lonely since Mohan left, she misses him.

'I will make sabzi and daal,' Jabeen tells her guest. 'I won't add garlic or onions either.'

Kokilaben smiles. 'I will stay, but only if you let me make you a Gujarati meal. You know, I am not allowed to cook in my own house. My maharaj gets upset if I try to help him,' she says with a sigh. 'He gets annoyed even if I enter the kitchen for something, he feels I am trespassing on his territory.'

'*Ji bilkul.* It will be a treat for us!' says Jabeen, genuinely delighted.

'I used to enjoy cooking. We will make daal dhokri together, our comfort food. With rotis made our way, thin and with a light spread of ghee. You people make your rotis too thick,' Kokilaben says.

'Yes, please.' It is Seema who has piped up.

'Do you have toover daal in the house?' Kokilaben asks.

'Toover?'

Seema comes to the rescue, 'It's arhar daal, Ammi.'

'Lots of it,' Jabeen says. 'We are not Punjabis; in our part it is our favourite daal.'

Kokilaben phones the driver and tells him to wait.

While the two women get to work, Seema stands by the kitchen door in amusement, not knowing what to make of the scene before her. Meanwhile, her brother has returned from his tuition and gone straight to his room.

Jabeen brings out a steel container of arhar daal and shows it to Kokilaben. She takes a handful and smells it.

'Perfect,' she says.

She puts several handfuls in a pot and tells Seema to wash it under the tap and let it soak. The visitor asks for various ingredients. No problem, Jabeen has them all. She volunteers to help with the rotis. She finishes kneading the flour she had abandoned earlier. Kokilaben joins her on the floor, sitting on a low stool. She makes several attempts with the belan before she is satisfied with the thinness of the rotis.

'I haven't done this in years,' she says wistfully, 'but I haven't lost the touch.'

She turns to Seema. 'Beti, leave us old ladies alone. Go watch television.'

The two are in no hurry. They are having a great time.

Seema goes down to the street and returns with half dozen little clay pots of phirnee from one of the shops.

'How is it going?' she asks when she returns.

Jabeen is gently stirring the daal pot with the dhokari pieces now floating in it.

'Fine, beta, just two old ladies reminiscing about their younger days,' Jabeen says.

'This is a simple hearty village meal,' Kokilaben says. 'My maharaj always makes a mess of it by adding too many unnecessary things.'

Jabeen tells Seema to start laying the small dining table in the living room.

Seema lays a tablecloth and brings out the plates and the katoris. She takes a plate of food for Rashid in his room.

'Who is she?' Rashid asks.

'Never mind,' she says. 'Have this. You'll like it.'

After some time, Rashid comes from his room.

'Can I have some more, please? I'm hungry and this is so tasty,' he says.

Kokilaben is delighted.

'Come here, son,' she says, and when Rashid does, she rises to kiss him on the forehead. Then she ladles some daal into his katori.

'Thank you, Aunty,' Rashid says, and joins them at the table.

Kokilaben has two phirnees as Seema clears the plates.

'Can I come again?' the visitor says at the door as she is leaving.

'We would like that very much,' Jabeen replies.

The two women hug.

Seema goes down with Kokilaben and escorts her to the car.

20

Mohan is glad his father chose Parsons. He likes being in New York, a city that's bursting with energy. In his second semester, he drops fashion design and signs up for a course that's more focused on the technical aspects of the business, import and export policies, safety standards at production centres.

It is a wise decision. He feels more confident, overcomes his shyness and becomes an enthusiastic participant in class discussions. He is the only student in the course from South Asia and the teachers encourage him to share his experiences in the garment trade in the region.

Mohan has five classes a week that last about an hour each. Sometimes the classes are in the evening, when people in the trade come as guest lecturers. Most of these men and women are from the city's garment district that is less than one square mile in the heart of Manhattan. It stretches from 34th Street to 42nd Street and lies between Fifth and Ninth avenues. The place is home to many showrooms and numerous major fashion labels. K&M has had business dealings with some of these companies in the past.

Mohan is delighted when one of the lecturers invites the students to take a tour, with him as a guide, one Saturday morning when the place will be largely deserted. The district has a sordid history. The lecturer tells them the place started as the source for cheap clothes for slaves working on plantations in the South.

'The glory days of this place are over,' Mr Rosenthal tells the students. 'The rents here have skyrocketed, it is no longer affordable for this line of business. Besides, we can't compete with manufacturers abroad in countries like Vietnam and Bangladesh where rents and labour are cheaper.'

He does not mention India to avoid embarrassing Mohan.

With time, Mohan begins to feel almost happy. He still misses home, especially his mother. And he misses Seema. But the mundane rhythms of life are taking over, calming him. In the evenings he often eats at restaurants close to home or picks up a packed meal, dosa and idli joints being his favourites. When he gets a craving for Gujarati food, he takes the bus from Parsons to the restaurant in midtown Manhattan recommended by Amrita. He is surprised by its popularity among the locals, until his friends tell him that vegetarian cuisine is becoming increasing popular in America, especially among the urban youth.

He watches television till past midnight and wakes up late. When he feels horny, he turns to one of the porno channels and is astounded at what is permissible in America.

Hamilton and Mohan have become friends and on weekends they explore the city together. Hamilton too is fairly new to New York. He grew up in Fort Lauderdale in Florida where his parents lived after winning a 'green card' in a lottery run by the State Department. He studied in a community college since that was all his parents could afford.

The mother is a home maker and the father is employed in the kitchen of a cruise ship.

One Sunday Mohan and Hamilton go to Bear Mountain State Park, close to the city, for a picnic. They travel partly by train and then by bus. The following weekend they go to the Cloisters Museum at the northern tip of Manhattan. It is a long ride and it is their way of seeing Harlem without getting off the bus.

Both have monthly passes that are valid for the bus as well as subway with no limits on the number of rides. Soon after arriving Mohan had learnt that there is one fixed fare on New York City public transport however long the ride.

The two see it all, they take the view from the top on Empire State building as well as the Statue of Liberty. Once, Hamilton takes his friend across the Hudson to the Gujarati ghetto in Edison for Sunday brunch. Their trip to Coney Island in Brooklyn is a disappointment. Mohan finds the smell of burnt meat on barbeque grills overpowering and unpleasant.

Late one evening Mohan is watching a sitcom on television—a rerun of his favorite, *Seinfeld*—while eating a Chinese takeout straight from the container with the plastic fork that came with it. The front doorbell rings. He checks his watch and is surprised someone is calling on him at this hour. It is Hamilton and he buzzes him in.

When Hamilton appears at his door he is trailed by Barbara and John. By the look on their faces, he realizes that something is amiss. It is Barbara who speaks.

'We're sorry for disturbing you so late, Mohan,' she says

and comes to the point right away, 'I have bad news. Your father passed away about two hours ago.'

Mohan is stunned but before he can react the husband and wife leave so that he can mourn privately. Hamilton has instructions to stay the night. As soon as the door closes, Mohan breaks down.

When he composes himself, he calls his mother. It will be early in the morning in Delhi. When she answers her cell phone, she just weeps, unable to say a word. Mohan consoles her as best as he can and tells her he is coming home. He tells his mother to put off the final rites till his arrival.

Mr Saxena is at their home, as Mohan knows he will be, and his mother hands the phone to him after a while. Mohan instructs the manager to buy a one-way ticket from New York for him on the first available non-stop flight to Delhi.

A few hours later an email arrives from Mr Saxena giving details of his booking on the next United Airlines flight leaving for Delhi from Newark. All he has to do is turn up at check-in two hours before the flight.

Barbara comes to the flat in the afternoon to take him to the airport. Mohan had arrived with a suitcase in New York. He has made acquisitions since and that morning had gone and bought a large duffle bag from a street vendor to put in the extras. It is cheap but sturdy. It will survive the journey and Mohan can discard it afterwards. The business class baggage allowance is generous. On a happier occasion he would have bought gifts for his family and friends.

Once the bags are in the car Barbara instructs Hamilton to go to Mr Park and settle any outstanding dues. She tells Mohan not to worry, she will settle with him later, not a problem.

'Thank you,' he tells her, misty eyed, as he leaves for the airport in the hired limousine.

'My family will wait for you to return,' she says, knowing that this is probably unlikely.

By the time the plane lands, it is past midnight. Mohan is jetlagged and is relieved that his mother is asleep. The family doctor has sedated her. The mother and son meet in the morning. By now Kokilaben is composed; she has accepted the loss.

Accompanied by Saxena, Mohan brings the body home from the morgue. Mr Saxena has advised most of the staff not to come to condole. There will be an occasion for that soon. Some close relatives have flown in from Gujarat.

A diya is lit near the head of the deceased and incense is burning. The priest ties a cloth under the chin and over the top of the head. The thumbs are tied together as are the two toes. Kokilaben breaks down when the body is lifted by Mohan and his cousins to be taken away in a hearse. She follows the Gujarati custom of women not attending the cremation. Mohan tries telling his mother that times have changed but she will not be persuaded.

The factory is closed for the day and the staff turns up in large numbers at the crematorium near Lodhi Road, as do other people who have known Kantibhai over the years. The family has opted for an open pyre with logs instead of an electric cremation. Kantibhai would have preferred that. Afterwards, a line is formed to offer condolences to Mohan and his close male relatives.

Later that afternoon Madhu and Seema come to sit with Kokilaben. It is a small gathering of close relatives, all of them leaving their shoes outside and sitting on the floor on gaddas. Kokilaban signals the two to come and sit next to her. There is little to be said. Afterwards, Madhu and Seema spend time with Mohan on the lawns, again not saying much. Mohan and Seema had parted badly and they are meeting again after almost a year. But the solemnity of the occasion takes away most of the awkwardness between them.

Mohan sends an email to the administration at Parsons informing them that he will not be completing his course. He only has a little more than a month left, but he cannot bear to leave his mother alone at a time like this.

On the fourth day there is a besanu, the Gujarati memorial service for the deceased. A small delegation of priests from a Gujarati sect has come to persuade the family to hold the service at their temple, on the banks of the Yamuna, but Mohan courteously declines. He decides to hold it at a more liberal Hindu centre on Lodhi Road.

Announcements of the prayer meeting have already appeared that morning in Delhi's two major newspapers. The Gujarati Samaj of Delhi circulates the information through e-mail and cell phones. Kantibhai was a highly respected member of the city's Gujarati community, a generous contributor to its welfare activities, and they turn up in large numbers.

Mohan takes charge at the factory but does not move into his father's larger office. It is turned into a conference room with a garlanded portrait of the old man prominently displayed. He installs a state-of-the-art video projection system as well as facilities for long distance conferencing.

He also builds a new cabin for his mother on the same

floor and encourages her to visit the office as often as she can. She is reluctant in the beginning but takes to it after a while. It helps her get over her depression. Soon, with Mohan's encouragement, the women on the staff drop in to chat with her whenever she is around. Kokilaben has a kind word for everyone. After a few weeks, she starts making an occasional round of the offices and the factory floor to understand the business better.

Mohan puts his Parsons studies to good use. His time in New York has helped him understand the American market better. The factory has been turning in a good profit since the government liberalized the industry, doing away with much of the licensing regulations. He sets a minimum wage for the manual workers on machines, considerably higher than the official minimum wage. He installs a medical unit with a full-time nurse and a general practitioner visiting every Friday. The workers on the factory floor are allowed to bring their children for consultation.

These good business practices do not go unnoticed among the garment importers abroad who have been under pressure from the media and NGOs not to do business in Third World countries where workers are exploited.

Mohan does some asking around among people he met at Parsons and obtains the services of an agent in the garment district in New York on the understanding that he can represent other companies as long as K&M is his sole client in India. The agent is paid a monthly retainer as well as commission on whatever new business he brings in.

An illustrated catalogue is designed to promote sales abroad. Mohan sends the prototype to the agent for comments. Several suggested changes are made and five hundred copies are printed on glossy paper. The agent sends it around to small clothing stores in malls around the country and with Mohan's permission, quotes prices lower than the cost of producing the dresses, packing and shipping them. The idea is to entice buyers into placing their first orders, and it works. The stores are impressed by the quality of work, the attractive packaging and more subtle colours than those of other Indian and Bangladeshi competitors.

The catalogues lead to a problem that Mohan had not foreseen. His designs are stolen and copied. But he soon learns to stay ahead of the plagiarists.

K&M receives a call from Sunil Lodha, owner of a chain of stores in Delhi as well as Mumbai, Bangalore and Ahmedabad. Mohan does not know him well, having met him only a few times at trade gatherings. But he agrees to meet the man.

Sunil Lodha's family has been making ayurvedic medicines for several generations. Over the years the company got burdened with too many cousins seeking managerial positions in the company. One day the elders decided to sack the lot and pass on the day-to-day running to professionals. The extended family would only have seats on the board of the company and share profits.

Sunil was one of the victims of the night of long knives. He decided to branch out into something entirely different. He used his bail out money and a loan from the bank to set up Band Baaja, a chain of shops in malls that would specialize in wedding wear, mostly for brides but also a selection for bridegrooms.

The shops were limited to four cities, Delhi, Mumbai,

Bangalore and Ahmedabad. They were targeted, essentially, at Indians living abroad with a wedding in the family coming up. To prepare for it they turn up in the home country to shop, knowing they are guaranteed a wider selection and cheaper shopping than wherever they are settled.

These shoppers from abroad have limited time on their hands and, most times, they fly in during the winter breaks in schools, at Christmas time, to shop for a wedding planned in spring when the weather in the West improves.

Sunil has a gimmick that works brilliantly. The shoppers can choose designs from samples on racks in the shops, the sales staff take measurements and the buyer can pick up the order after seven days. The delivery time is guaranteed or the buyer gets his money back and the outfit is handed over free with the compliments of the management. If necessary, the company will also courier dresses abroad at no extra cost to the customer.

The problem is that the business is seasonal. During the rest of the year a lot depends on the alignment of celestial bodies for the setting up of wedding dates. The result is that factory is underproducing for most of the year and the unions do not allow Sunil to employ seasonal labour. He is losing a fortune.

The meeting is set up at K&M on the visitor's request. Mohan suspects that he wanted to see his operation but, in reality, Sunil does not wish to inconvenience Mohan by asking him to come all the way to Gurgaon.

'I have a proposition for you,' Sunil cuts to the chase at his first meeting with Mohan. People are sometimes put off by Sunil's no-nonsense approach to discussions, an American habit he picked up at Wharton.

'I'm listening,' Mohan says, pushing the plate of Oreo biscuits towards Sunil as they have coffee.

'I'm overstretched,' Sunil says, 'I can't meet the demands of the franchises across the country. I shouldn't have expanded so widely. In the busy season, my factory operates around the clock and the overtime payments are killing me. Rest of the year the factory is underutilized.'

'What do have you in mind?' Mohan wants to know.

'I want to close down my factory altogether and concentrate on sales. I want your company to produce the outfits for me with my label and I will take it from there.'

Mohan realizes that the man has done his homework. The output at K&M slows down in the winter season. He can easily absorb the extra orders coming his way from Sunil.

'I will discuss this with my people and get back to you,' Mohan says.

Truth be told, Mohan has already decided. The deal is done and papers signed within days. The returns are almost immediate.

With money rolling in, Mohan builds a school close to the factory in memory of his father. In the compound there is a crèche that he names after his mother. Kokilaben finds a vocation. She spends time with the pre-school children, playing with them and teaching them the basics while the mothers are at work.

22

Madhu completes almost four years with K&M, having moved up the ladder rapidly to become chief of the exports section. A head-hunter approaches her discreetly and makes a tempting offer. She has already decided it is time to move.

First, she researches the company that wants to employ her. Indian Shades is a major garment producing house, internationally renowned, with good business practices. It specializes in ethnic wear for both men and women, exclusively cotton, most of it handloom. It places orders with weavers in the villages. To encourage the poor, it gives interest-free loans to get them started and over the years has built schools for their children as well as health clinics for the families. The seriously ill are sent to hospitals and specialists at company expense.

Indian Shades provides designs and colours to the weavers that suit the urban elite as well as customers abroad who shun polyester. When the buyers of shops that cater to this market turn up in Delhi they are taken to the villages and given a presentation. They are suitably impressed.

While benevolent, the company is also a hard taskmaster. It demands consistency from the loom owners and gets it. Otherwise, it walks away. There are no middlemen to cut the earnings of the workers, everything is bought from them directly. What attracts Madhu is that these craftspeople are encouraged to own equity in the company at a generous discount.

The company intends to expand into producing dhurries, handwoven shawls, handcrafted jewellery, as well as furniture and home furnishings. That is where Madhu comes in; the company needs more hands on the management side, particularly in the field.

'You will be posted in Jaisalmer in Rajasthan,' the chair of the interview panel tells her. 'Does that work for you?'

'Yes, Ma'am.'

'There will be no fixed nine-to-five hours. Your salary will reflect that.'

Madhu has no problem with that either.

Madhu is excited by the offer but she asks for a few days to think it over. This will involve a major change in her life and she wants to first discuss the matter with her parents. As she suspected, her parents are none too pleased.

'Beta, why leave Delhi? You have so many friends here and you are doing so well professionally,' her mother says.

It is left unsaid that Madhu is now of marriageable age, in fact, by the standards of her community, she should have been married three or four years ago.

Madhu's father does not say anything, he is a man of few words. But Madhu knows he is unhappy with the development that has taken them both by surprise.

'Maa, there is no future in the company I work for,' Madhu says. 'I have risen as far as I can go. This offer is challenging. If it works out, I will ask them to transfer me to their main office in Delhi after a couple of years.'

The parents are not convinced but they let it go. They have a sensible daughter whose judgement they trust. Madhu is approaching her late twenties now, but they know that their daughter will have no difficulty finding a husband outside their tradition bound, conservative community. It can be a good thing.

When Madhu meets Seema over coffee and tells her, the friend is more understanding.

'I envy you,' she says.

'Come visit me once I settle down.'

'Try and stop me!'

When Madhu submits her resignation, Mohan is sorry to see her go. He knows better than to try persuading her to stay. He gives her a generous bonus as a parting gift.

The customary farewell is arranged for her in the cafeteria on her last day. To Madhu's surprise, Kokilaben turns up. Before she leaves, Madhu bends down and touches her feet. More than Mohan, it is Kokilaben she will miss.

Madhu flies to Jaisalmer on the first day of the following month. Her mother wants to travel with her to settle the daughter down and keep her company for the first few days. Her father dissuades her; she will only get in the way.

'Maa, you and Papa must come and visit after I have a place of my own,' Madhu says tearfully.

The company puts her at Fort Rajwada Hotel while the bungalow on the plains that has been leased for her is being furnished. Madhu was hoping to reside within the magnificent fort itself, believed to be among the oldest forts in the world, within which people still live day-to-day lives. The massive structure was built in the twelfth century amidst the sandy expense of the Thar. It stood at the crossroads of major trade routes, including the silk route. Madhu soon realizes how impractical the idea of living in that chaos really is.

Soon enough a truckload of her personal belongings arrives from Delhi. A small army of men do the unpacking, more supervisors than actual unpackers. A few days later she adopts a puppy, a stray, to keep her company.

The yellow sandstone bungalow is on two levels. The ground floor rooms will be the office while the floor above will be her private quarters. A jeep and a driver will be at her disposal around the clock. The driver has his quarters behind the bungalow.

Her assignment will require travelling and occasionally spending the nights in small towns and villages in a hotel, if there is one, or in a tent that will go with her, tucked away at the back of the jeep.

After several interviews, she employs a middle-aged, childless widow as her domestic help. Gopi is tried out for a few days and Madhu likes her; she is woman of few words and good at cooking vegetarian dishes.

Since Gopi will have time on her hands taking care of just one person, she is willing to sweep and dust the house as well. As for the laundry, Madhu is alarmed when she sees Gopi thrashing the clothes with a wooden bat, a thaapi, that came with the house. Madhu teaches her to use the washing machine. The servant's room is next to the kitchen, with a bed and attached bathroom. It is Gopi's private area, something new for her and something she cherishes.

After a week she tells Madhu shyly that she is good at massaging, having learnt it at her previous job.

'That's great, Didi,' her employer says, 'My skin has become dry since I got her. A massage once or twice a week will be nice.'

The maid blushes at being addressed as 'didi' by the younger woman.

And unlike her previous employers Madhu has not enquired about her caste.

Ashish Kumar, who had run the operation single-handed until Madhu's arrival, feels threatened by her at first, but Madhu assures him that he is indispensable to the company.

'Ashish ji, I am new here,' she tells him. 'You are practically a local, you know all the people here. I will need your guidance.'

He accompanies her on tours of the villages and Madhu notices that he is well liked by the weavers. It is the women who work at the looms, while their husbands till their small parcels of land or work as labourers on daily wage. The weaving brings them a little extra income for household expenses and sometimes they splurge, buying electricity connections and installing running water.

Soon Madhu has the confidence to venture out alone with the driver and leaves Ashish to take care of the office. If it is lunchtime the women invite her to eat with them and she politely declines, knowing that they are hardly in a position to feed another mouth. But she will gladly accept a cup of tea.

Seema comes to visit for a week in the early stages of winter. Madhu takes her on her rounds to show her the misery that plagues the lives of most of the people in the villages. One Friday, in one of the villages with a sizeable Muslim population, Seema joins the women at noon prayer, much to their delight.

One evening they join a tourist group, a mix of Indians and foreigners, for a trip to the sand dunes forty kilometres from the fort, lying deep in the grandeur of the Thar. They travel in cramped jeeps that don't miss a single pothole. Along the way they sight the great Indian bustard and chinkaras.

Carpets are laid out on the sand and they sit and watch the sun go down. Soon a retinue of servants arrives in a van with food, tents and supplies.

As it gets dark, a bonfire is lit and the group listen to Sufi songs in local dialects. The musicians play wooden instruments and cymbals. The guests are entertained with folk dances passed down generations, mainly the ghoomar of the Rajputs, performed by women in colourful ghagra and cholis. They swirl sensuously but keep their faces covered with veils.

The concluding piece is the bhavai dance with women balancing as many as nine earthen pots—Seema counts—on their heads and twirling their feet on brass plates while their husbands sing and play harmoniums, sarangis and dholaks. Seema and Madhu sit so mesmerised by the grand finale that they forget to take pictures.

It is a little past nine when waiters bring drinks—potent local brews—and beer. When bhang is circulated the girls take sips, a new experience. Everyone is famished by the time the food is laid on a buffet table. There is laal maas, the fiery local mutton curry, as well as vegetarian dishes like gatte ki sabji, steamed gram flour dumplings in gravy, dahi boondi and hot, freshly baked rotis.

The evening is remarkably cool, with an occasional breeze. The camels grunt and gurgle in contentment. As the fires are put out, everyone goes to bed in shared tents. It is getting cold but the blankets are heavy.

Most times, though, they remain in Jaisalmer. Seema is happy relaxing in the house while Madhu gets on with her work. Sometimes she goes for a walk and is pleased that the men do not stare at women in the streets the way they do in Delhi. She discards her dupatta for the rest of her stay. The place has a small-town feel. With a touch of guilt, she relishes the joy of being away from home.

After a few days she dumps her stuff in the guest bedroom and sleeps on the double bed in Madhu's room, under a shared duvet. They talk late into the night with the winds howling outside. The small electric heater is of little use in the desert's cold night.

The two remember their college days, friends they had forgotten, Seema's job hunting in a hijab, the deception at the interview with Kantibhai. It all seems like such a long time ago. They laugh and giggle as the memories flood in.

One evening they light a bonfire in the garden and invite Madhu's newfound friends for dinner. To Seema's surprise Madhu opens beer bottles for the guests.

'You've come a long way, girl!' Seema whispers to her. Her friend grins.

On Seema's final night in Jaisalmer, Madhu tells her about her boyfriend.

A few months before Seema's visit, on a Sunday afternoon Madhu had taken the jeep to the war museum constructed by the Desert Corps during the Raj. It was more out of boredom than anything else. The place was a short distance away on the highway to Jodhpur.

There were few visitors and Madhu, in the company of four other tourists, was taken around by a young army officer who was on guide duty that day. The exhibit included vehicles and equipment used by the army during its operations against Pakistan some decades earlier. The names of winners of gallantry awards during that brief war were engraved in granite on one wall. Someone, perhaps a relative of a deceased, had laid a bouquet of marigolds next to the wall.

There was a Hunter Aircraft that destroyed enemy tanks in the Battle of Longewala. It was a short tour.

Some days later, an engraved invitation was hand delivered to Madhu's residence. It was from the local Member of Parliament inviting her to dinner at his home, a short distance from the fort. Madhu had of course heard of him but was somewhat surprised that the man was even aware of her existence.

The card was ridiculously large, the lettering was in gold and the MP's background and achievements, such as they were, were mentioned in detail on the reverse. The invitation was to a 'gala party' to celebrate the man's birthday.

'I have no intention of going,' Mahu told Ashish.

'But you must,' he said, 'he's very powerful here and he can be helpful to us.'

'Why is he inviting *me*?' she asked.

'He must have heard that you are popular with his constituents. You can help him get some votes.'

'All the more reason for not going.'

'That's not a good idea,' Ashish advised her, 'He'll be offended and might make things difficult for us.'

Ashish helped Madhu pick a kurta from the stocks as a birthday present for the host, having a fairly good idea what would fit the man but also knowing that it would end up in the cupboard of one of his servants.

When Madhu reached the MP's bungalow the next evening, men in uniform with guns at the entrance gate checked her name against a list before the jeep was let in.

The party was held on the lawns. Madhu joined a queue of guests waiting to be greeted by the birthday boy. Most of them were holding bouquets of flowers that the host accepted and passed on to one of his employees who, in turn, placed them on an ever-growing pile. Now it occurred to Madhu that flowers might have been a better idea than the kurta. When it was her turn to be introduced, she was greeted a bit too effusively. The MP had done his homework.

'Welcome to Jaisalmer, Madhu ji,' he said looking over her shoulder to see who was next in line, 'please get in touch with me if there is anything I can do for you while you are with us.'

'Thank you, sir,' she said as she handed him the birthday gift.

The spacious lawns were lit up and Bollywood music was playing loudly. There was a band that Madhu learned later had flown in from Delhi. She strolled around with a glass of fresh juice to see if there was someone she recognized, anyone she could cling to before some bore or chatterbox approached her.

The food had not yet been laid out but a small army of servants were busy bringing the dishes from the kitchen. Ashish had warned her that dinner would not be served till at least eleven. Madhu had no intention of waiting till then, and had begun planning an exit without being noticed.

'Hello, Ma'am,' she heard someone say.

She turned around and there was a young man, about her age, with a smile. She couldn't place him.

'Perhaps you don't remember me. I was your guide at the war museum,' he said.

'Yes, of course,' Madhu said, extending her hand. 'Sorry, I did not recognize you. You are not in your uniform. I am Madhu.'

'I'm Vijay, it's nice to meet you again.'

He spoke English with a sing-song accent that gave away his provincial background. Madhu liked that.

Vijay told her he knew nobody at the party. 'But then technically I was not even invited,' he confessed.

'Don't tell me you're gatecrashing,' she said mischievously.

'No, not like that,' Vijay said, 'the Brigadier in charge of the local military station was invited and asked me to come along to keep him company. His wife doesn't care for such parties.'

'I'm glad I met you,' Madhu said, 'I was about to leave. I've been in town only a few months and I too don't know anyone here.'

Now Madhu decided to stay a bit longer than she had earlier intended. When dinner was announced they moved to the long buffet tables. They were the early birds. To Madhu's delight, there was a chaat station with bhel puri, vadas, even golgappas. She told the server to warm up two aloo tikkis. She hadn't had any since leaving Delhi. Vijay had intended to head for the separate area that held the meat dishes but he decided to stay with Madhu.

'I think I should be on my way,' Madhu said, as they finished their food. 'I'm so glad I bumped into you again.'

He insisted on accompanying her to her jeep.

'We are having a small farewell party in the officers' mess on Friday for one of our friends who is being posted out,' he told her, 'I would like to invite you if you are free.'

Madhu hesitated.

'There will be ladies there, most of them wives of officers,' he quickly added, 'I'm one of the very few bachelors.'

'I would love to come,' Madhu said. 'Send me the details and let me know the dress code.'

He gave her a missed call on her mobile number.

'See you then,' she said.

'Wonderful,' said Vijay.

She loved his smile.

At the farewell party for the departing officer, the two of them danced to old, slow Bollywood songs. She was a little high, and very happy. He smelt good, his breath on her neck and his arm around her waist felt good.

23

Seema moves from the bank in Gurgaon to a different one in New Delhi following an offer from a headhunter she cannot refuse. She is now the deputy head of HR at an American bank whose customers are mostly international businesses with offices in the National Capital Region. A few embassies also bank with it. It is what one can call a boutique bank and not everyone can open an account there.

Seema's salary is good and she now lives in Zakir Bagh in Okhla with her mother and brother, a safer locality for Muslims than the conflict-prone old city. Named after a former President of India, the colony has a couple of hundred flats originally intended for minority communities, Muslims as well as Christians. About ninety per cent of the residents are still Muslim. It is a comfortable, clean area with wide roads and trees. Jabeen, however, misses the camaraderie of their old place, the sounds and bustle of the gali.

Rashid is now an equal partner in a shop that sells and repairs computers in the main square of Nehru Place. The other partner is the investor and Rashid runs the shop on his own. Jabeen is always urging him to get married—there have been a series of proposals—but the boy, like his sister, is in no hurry. He does not let on that he will not marry until his elder sister is settled. The family is comfortable and happy and Javed no longer nags his sister about her daughter's future. He is secretly proud of what his niece and nephew have achieved.

Seema comes to the office by car and parks in the basement in a space allotted to senior management. As has become her habit these days, she is smartly dressed in a pant suit. Her hair is shorter, she has lipstick on and carries a briefcase to work. There is a confident swagger in the young woman.

The hijab is still there.

As she presses the lift button her phone rings. She checks the caller and smiles.

'Hi Mohan.'

'Hi. What are you doing this Saturday?' he asks.

'Madhu is in town for a few days. Her parents have invited me for dinner,' she tells him.

'Tell Madhu to invite me also,' he pleads.

'Nope,' she says, 'we intend to gossip and you won't fit in.'

'I rang up because Baa wants you and your mother to come for lunch on Sunday.'

Seema looks at her watch as the lift arrives. She still has time.

'Tell Baa we would love to come. I'll check with Ammi, I'm sure it is fine with her.'

Seema realizes that, for the first time, she has addressed Mohan's mother as 'Baa' without intending to. She blushes.

'Tell Aunty to make that daal. Ammi can't stop talking about it, but tell her to go easy on the sugar. Ammi is now borderline diabetic.'

The office is swank. No unnecessary files, no clutter. What you don't need has to be kept in the locker assigned to you. Everyone is expected to be smartly dressed. The American branch manager is particular about such things. Seema heads for her corner cabin. It is five minutes to opening time.

She greets her colleagues, sits down and fires up her computer.

Madhu and Vijay's wedding takes place with great dhoom-dhaam. The parents splurge on their only child. Once she had reached a certain age, they were ready to accept any boy as a groom, besides which, their daughter was determined not to have an arranged marriage. As it turned out, they took an immediate liking to Vijay.

Vijay's regiment, the Dogra Regiment, traces its lineage as far back as 1858. It is a tradition in the family to have the oldest son serve in the army. Vijay's father, now retired, was an army man in the same regiment while Vijay's grandfather served with the British forces in the Second World War in Italy. Before him an ancestor took part in the offensive against the Turks and saw action in the decisive Battle of Megiddo in what was then Palestine. He received a gallantry award. Captain Vijay Dogra is the first in the family with officer rank. Before him they were all foot soldiers.

Vijay's ancestral home is a village, Shakargarh, on the banks of a stream that originates in the hills of Jammu. His family still have relatives there and visit them for occasions like weddings and cremations. As a boy, Vijay's father Tikamgarh used to ride a mare to and from school which was in a nearby mofussil town several kilometres away.

When the father retired from the army the family decided

to settle in Dharampur, a small town in the Solan district of Himachal Pradesh, close to Dagshai, the cantonment of his last posting. As luck would have it their new home was close to a posh boarding school, more than a hundred years old. The British had built it for children of their middle-ranking army officers who could not afford to send their children to boarding schools in England. After Independence, it was Indianized and catered mainly to children whose parents had once attended such schools, as well as children who were problematic at home.

In the spirit of good neighbourliness, the school offered full scholarships to two local boys every year who were admitted as day students. The teachers were kind and saw to it that these lads from the hills kept up with the rest of the class, but the boarders from posh homes on the plains were not so kind. They ragged these boys mercilessly and made fun of their rustic ways.

Vijay, who was awarded one of the scholarships, was miserable the four years he was in the school, but in the final exams he topped the class. The proud father saw to it that Vijay went to a college in Chandigarh, two hours away from Dharampur. Vijay stayed in the college hostel and returned home on Fridays for the weekend. After graduation he applied for admission to the National Defence Academy and was accepted immediately because of his family's military lineage. He was a natural for the Dogra regiment. Jaisalmer station was his second posting.

Madhu and Vijay got on splendidly after the initial awkwardness. When he proposed to her a few months after they met, she had been expecting it.

It's a Sunday morning in late December. The date was chosen keeping in mind the school winter break because the children of Vijay's relatives in the hills didn't want to miss out on a trip to the capital as well as the festivities.

By now Vijay is posted at the Mhow cantonment, close to Indore. It is essentially a place where new recruits to the army, officers as well as the infantry, are trained. Captain Vijay Dogra oversees the army museum there. The Lieutenant General in command makes some calls and gets permission for the wedding ceremony and the reception to be held inside Delhi Cantonment. The Guptas are pleased. It saves them the headache of finding a wedding hall somewhere beyond the walls of the cramped Old City.

The neighbours and relatives of the Guptas are impressed, few have been this far out of the old city. They come in shared and rented cars. Kokilaben and Mohan are invited but Mohan is out of the country on pressing business and his mother is uncomfortable attending alone. They have sent a wedding gift.

The ceremony is held in the morning in the Dogra tradition and limited to relatives and close friends. During the ritual Uma insists that Seema sit next to her daughter as the bridesmaid, an honour denied to her cousins. Their mothers are more upset than the girls. They bitch for a while before letting the matter drop.

Vijay has booked as many rooms as available in the cantonment. His parents and closest relatives stay in them with extra beds brought in for the children. Two of the rooms are kept unoccupied as changing rooms and to let elderly guests rest between the ceremony and lunch that is outdoors on the spacious lawns under a tent. Drinks are served and the Guptas insist on paying for that as well. They come from the cantonment canteen, much cheaper than in shops. The Lieutenant-General in Mhow, pulling rank, has arranged for that.

The buffet spreads are on both sides of the bar. The vegetarian dishes are prepared by a halwai from old Delhi who has brought all his cooking paraphernalia: handis, tawas, vegetables and cooks. The non-vegetarian food comes from the cantonment kitchen: kebabs, meat curries and biryani.

The disc jockey starts with western numbers but there are few takers, except for some army retirees who try out their skills at the fox trot and waltz. When the jockey turns to Bollywood numbers the dance floor fills up and soon there is no room to swing a cat. Everyone is on the floor, the young and the old, some mothers carrying their babies, fathers dancing with their daughters. Seema looks on, too shy to join in, until she feels a familiar hand on her shoulder. She looks up. It is Mohan. He has taken an early flight back and persuaded Kokilaben to get into a sari and come.

Mohan takes Seema's hand and they begin to move together. It seems as if their bodies fit, their rhythms match. Kokilaben and Jabeen look at each other. They smile. The men have had it their way for too long; now it is time for them to have their say. They do not need to say it. It will happen. Those two young bodies moving in unison are speaking to each other.

Vijay and Madhu spend the night in the VIP guest room of the cantonment, not too exhausted by the events of the day.

Epilogue

Two years on, Seema and Mohan have a civil marriage at the Chattarpur farmhouse that Kantibhai had built. A sub-registrar of marriages is persuaded to come all the way from his office in Jamnagar House in New Delhi. It a brief affair, the two sign a marriage document. Some relatives have sent their regrets while some have not bothered to respond to the invitation.

The gathering is small. Uncle Javed, now a widower, has come with his two grown up sons, as have Kokilaben's sister and her husband from Ahmedabad. Amrita, as she had promised Mohan, has flown in with Paul. Their six-month-old daughter is taking a nap in one of the bedrooms upstairs after polishing off a jar of Gerber's baby food brought from New York. One can't be too careful. She is under the watchful eyes of a local ayah.

Amrita is in a silk saree, one of many she has inherited from her mother. Paul is wearing a bespoke kurta designed by Rohit Bal that comes with a turban. It is not a yarmulke but his Orthodox Jewish parents in Brooklyn will be pleased when he sends them photographs and sees that his head is covered for the solemn occasion.

Madhu's parents were not on the original list of invitees but, through their daughter, they send word that they would like to attend. Kokilaben rings them and apologizes for the oversight; she ticks off her son for the lapse and has an invitation hand delivered.

Amrita and Madhu have the honour of signing the marriage document as witnesses. After that the two mothers, Jabeen and Kokilaben, join the waiters in serving the food to the guests on the tables, a Gujarati feast.

Seema and Mohan have agreed to adhere to their respective faiths. And they have agreed that if they have children, as they dearly hope they will, the kids will be exposed to the traditions and rituals of both Hinduism and Islam and it will be left to them to decide what religion they wish to follow, if any.

Mohan is in a Saville Row suit gifted by Sir Harold Sedley in London who sent his regrets. Seema is in a Dior dress, a Hermes scarf sent from New York by Barbara Elliot over her shoulders.

Kokilaben has worn a beautifully embroidered shirt with a gharara that she has borrowed from Jabeen. Jabeen is in one of Kokilaben's intricately woven patola sarees from Patan. Both sets are heirlooms in the families for generations.

It is their way of saying 'fuck you' to the world, though neither of them would have any idea what the words mean.

